WR1

Allie Kincheloe has been writing stories for as long as she can remember, and somehow they always become romances. Always a Kentucky girl at heart, she now lives in Tennessee with her husband, children, and a growing menagerie of pets. Visit her on Twitter: @AllieKAuthor.

Also by Allie Kincheloe

Heart Surgeon's Second Chance
A Nurse, a Surgeon, a Christmas Engagement
Reunited with Doctor Devereaux

Discover more at millsandboon.co.uk.

WINTER NIGHTS WITH THE SINGLE DAD

ALLIE KINCHELOE

MILLS & BOON

First published in Great Britain 2021
by Mills & Boon, an imprint of HarperCollins*Publishers* Ltd,
1 London Bridge Street, London, SE1 9GF

www.harpercollins.co.uk

HarperCollins*Publishers*
1st Floor, Watermarque Building,
Ringsend Road, Dublin 4, Ireland

Large Print edition 2022

Special thanks and acknowledgement are given to
Allie Kincheloe for her contribution
to The Christmas Project miniseries.

ISBN: 978-0-263-29380-7

05/22

MIX
Paper from
responsible sources
FSC® C007454

This book is produced from independently certified
FSC™ paper to ensure responsible forest management.
For more information visit www.harpercollins.co.uk/green.

Printed and Bound in the UK using 100% Renewable
Electricity at CPI Group (UK) Ltd, Croydon, CR0 4YY

For my amazing editors.

Some books come easily.

Others exist because of editors
who push flighty authors like me
to be better.

CHAPTER ONE

NERVES FLUTTERED IN Stella's stomach. Getting called to the boss's office was never easy, even when she was quite certain she'd done nothing wrong. She'd run through a litany of possibilities, but still she had no clue what else she could have been called in to discuss other than a potential promotion.

"Dr. Allen, you must've caught wind of some changes happening." The chair squeaked as Chris Taylor leaned back. The chief executive steepled his fingers and gazed at her with a serious expression lining his face. "And I'm sure you've questioned how these changes might affect your own role here at the hospital."

Whispers in the hallowed halls of the Royal Kensington Hospital said that the head of orthopedics could be replaced soon. Rumors floated rampant through the antiseptic-scented corridors since a nurse had caught sight of an employment ad for an orthopedic surgeon.

No one had mentioned retirement and none seemed on the verge of a big move, but Stella had sought out the advertisement and read it with her own eyes only an hour before she'd been pulled into Dr. Taylor's office. Her confidence flagged a bit and she barely resisted the urge to cross her fingers or pray that she wasn't about to be fired.

Stella nodded, waiting for Dr. Taylor to get on with it. The man was known for his long-winded explanations of any and every topic of conversation. Stella herself preferred to get to the point quickly and her foot shook as her impatience got the best of her.

"I realize this is your first year with us, so you may not be aware of the particulars. You have heard of The Kensington Project?"

Thinking carefully, Stella nodded slowly. "I have, but only in the broadest of terms. Last year's participants had already returned from their assignments before I came on board here."

"Then you must know it's a medical exchange program of sorts. Four of our own, from various departments, will be traveling to other hospitals across the world to share our groundbreaking advancements. And you've been chosen to share your orthopedic techniques."

"Me?" Stella savored the moment of recognition. Out of all the doctors and surgeons in the elite programs at the Royal Kensington Hospital, she'd been chosen. What an honor! The validation of her surgical skills filled her with pride.

"Yes." Dr. Taylor passed her a file. "If you are agreeable, you would travel to Toronto. While you are there, you will work with the team at St. Matthew's Hospital until Christmas."

"Canada?" Stella gasped. "I've never been to Canada." Stella opened the folder in her lap. Scanning quickly, she tried to absorb as many of the details as possible. The particular that stood out most was that her departure date was within the week and the return date not until Christmas. "I'd be leaving almost immediately?"

"Afraid so. It's rather short notice, but I believe you to be up for the task." His face took on a more solemn demeanor. "There's one more thing."

Her breath caught as she waited for the bad

news that was sure to come with the concern lining his face. Good news always comes with bad, after all.

"In addition to sharing your surgical procedures, we've also secured permission for you to film that television special you've been angling for since your arrival here."

Stella's eyes widened at the news. "I'll be able to film there at St. Matthew's?"

Dr. Taylor nodded. "The producer will have a camera crew film here beginning next week and another to join you in Toronto. I don't seem to have an exact timeline on that. There are a few caveats as noted in the file, mostly legal minutiae that will apply. I'm sure you're familiar with most everything, but do review it for any differences applicable specifically to Toronto. Your contact there is going to be Dr. Aiden Cook. His information is also in the file."

Having grown up on camera, Stella knew the power film had on the general public and its opinion. She'd been trying to secure permission to document just how hard the people in a hospital worked and to bring attention to the sacrifices made to provide healthcare for the masses. Those sacrifices were amplified at the holidays, so she'd pitched the upcoming Christmas holiday as the perfect time for filming. She'd managed to get the support of a network, but getting permission from the hospital had been far more difficult as she'd been refused at every turn.

So, why now?

"Dr. Allen?"

"Hmm..." Stella fought back a blush at being caught woolgathering. "I'm afraid my mind was wandering."

"Are you agreeing to participate then?"

Momentarily, Stella wondered if she ought to decline. Had she only been chosen for the program due to her television background? No, she was quite confident in her surgical skills and the Royal Kensington Hospital would never send her out to represent their good name if they didn't believe in her. Plus, the topic of the show was one near and dear to her heart.

After the briefest of hesitations, Stella said yes.

She walked away from Dr. Taylor's office

deep in thought. Excitement filled her at all the prospects The Kensington Project offered. Her motivations for agreeing were threefold.

First of all, it was a wonderful career opportunity. She'd get to share her new techniques in another country and meet a whole new team of colleagues. Expanding her network could potentially open a lot of doors going forward.

Second, and most excitingly, it would put an ocean between Stella and her mother for two entire months. That alone would be reason enough for Stella to say yes. For years, Debra Allen had pushed and pushed to get Stella into television and keep her there. Stella had heard a million times how much her mum had wanted to be an actress, but she simply hadn't had the talent. She'd shoved all those dreams on to her daughter. Being in the spotlight, holding that hint of celebrity status, had often been all that mattered. Occasionally, Stella had wondered if it was her or what she could do for her mum that Debra loved more. She loved her mum, but a vast expanse of water separating them could only improve their relationship.

The third and final reason was that this television program meant everything to her. She'd been keen on getting this program produced for ages. The idea of filming had never been more exciting.

The feeling that her whole life was about to change filled Stella with energy. Mentally, she began listing all the tasks she needed to complete before she left London. There were a lot, so she really should make a written to-do list. She had packing to do before her first ever trip to Canada. Thankfully, she'd kept her passport up to date. She needed to sort her current patient load and arrange for someone to care for her houseplants.

Stella wasn't the sentimental type, but this felt right. It was going to be the best Christmas yet.

She couldn't wait.

Aiden groaned as he opened yet another email from Dr. Stella Allen, the surgeon from the Royal Kensington Hospital that he'd agreed to babysit—*liaise with*—while she was in Toronto. The things he'd do for his kid…

Emergency medicine at one of the busiest hospitals in Toronto wasn't meshing well with single fatherhood. He kept running late, having to rely on his parents to pick up the slack when his job kept him past the scheduled pickup time. The trade-off of coordinating with Dr. Allen on filming her television special and planning the staff Christmas party had seemed worth it in exchange for only working day shifts and no weekends through all of November and December. Now he was second-guessing that thought because she was already grating on his last nerve and they weren't even in the same country.

Dr. Allen had sent him no fewer than a dozen emails over the last twenty-four hours. And the questions? She asked more questions than anyone he'd ever met. And he hadn't even met her yet!

Something in this particular email caught his attention though. Dr. Allen wrote that she'd need to scout the hospital for places to film that would have enough lighting, yet not be too distracting on film. That wasn't the intriguing bit though. Helping her coordinate filming had been part of the deal he'd made with Dr. Stone, after all. It was the next line that sent him off on a research tangent.

She wrote that with several shows behind her, she could evaluate the locations with a glance.

Several shows?

Wasn't this a special one-time deal designed to highlight the struggles of those who worked in hospitals during the holidays? But her words implied she'd done more than this documentary.

He typed her name into the search bar and was not disappointed. Pages of results showed up for her. He settled back and began to work his way through a few of the links. It didn't take long for him to learn everything he needed to know about St. Matthew's newest star.

Dr. Allen had grown up in the spotlight. After an appearance on a show called *Britain's Brightest* at age ten, she had been given her own show—*Stay Smart with Stella.* After that, she had another show while she was in college and medical school.

She had taken time away from her studies to futz about with a television program during medical school and he was supposed to believe that she was one of the brightest pioneers the

Royal Kensington Hospital had to offer? Was there a time when she had ever focused all her attention on medicine? Could she really perform orthopedic surgery?

Aiden snorted. More likely, she was the one with the most star power to draw attention to their program.

And the most photogenic.

"Oh, she's pretty. Is she the one you're going to be showing around?"

"It's a bit more than showing her around, Mom," Aiden said as his mother leaned over his shoulder to look at the screen in his hand.

"Well, she's quite lovely. Is she single?"

"I don't know, but it doesn't matter. She's a colleague only."

His mom made a noise of disbelief. "You cannot be alone forever, Aiden. You know, if you found someone new, maybe she could help you shoulder some of the responsibilities."

"Jamie needs stability more than I need a love life, Mom." He resisted the urge to roll his eyes. He didn't have the time or the interest for romance. Where would he find the time? He'd had to bargain for extra duties to get regular hours for the next two months.

"Don't reject the idea before you've even met her." His mom smiled softly as she walked away. "And don't stay up too late."

He sighed. Soon, he and Jamie would need to find a place of their own, but for now, living with his parents was the most stability that Aiden could provide. His son had been through so much upheaval in the short duration of his life and the last thing Aiden wanted to do was add to that.

The low-battery message popped up and it dawned on him that he'd just lost over an hour educating himself about an actress masquerading as a doctor. Dr. Stella Allen was very beautiful and she had an on-air presence that made her seem as if she were talking directly to the viewer. The spark of intelligence in her green eyes lit so brightly that it was visible even on camera. The camera might add ten pounds, but if it did, they'd landed in just the right places on the curvy, dark-haired beauty. Something about her had drawn him in, even in a video. He ran a hand through his hair.

What was he doing?

Surely, he had learned his lesson about getting tangled up with actresses. The last thing he needed was another woman in his life more concerned about the camera than the people around her. Been there, done that, got the two-year-old to prove it.

Stepping across the hall, he watched from the doorway as Jamie slept. Even after months in Aiden's care, Jamie slept with his back to the wall curled up into a tight ball. Aiden still wasn't sure what his son had been through in the two years before Aiden had learned of his existence. Some days, just the thought of what it might have been was too much.

But that was in the past and Aiden was determined to give his son a better future. Jamie's appearance may have turned Aiden's life upside down, but being a dad was the best thing that had ever happened to him. These last nine months had meant a lot of changes for Aiden, including moving back in with his parents and trying to juggle Jamie's therapies and work and a massive custody battle. He had no regrets about stepping up when his son came into his life though. In fact, that little boy was the sole reason Aiden had gotten himself saddled with being a personal concierge for the next two months.

And he was also the reason that Aiden needed to keep Dr. Stella Allen at arm's length.

CHAPTER TWO

STELLA GLANCED AT her watch yet again. Her contact from St. Matthew's Hospital should have been there to pick her up an hour ago. She let out a deep sigh and took her nearly dead cell phone from her purse.

With a few taps she brought up the email she'd received from Dr. Cook confirming that they'd meet here at the airport. Her itinerary had been attached. She fired off a quick missive that her plane had landed and she was eagerly awaiting their arrival.

She hadn't thought to get his phone number and it was a bit too late for that now. Normally, she was far more organized than this, but since she'd only found out three days prior that she'd been selected to come to Toronto for the prestigious Kensington Project, she needed to give herself a bit of slack. She was still quite giddy about being chosen.

Of course, she'd have signed on for Antarctica if it allowed her to put an ocean between her and her parents for two solid months. Her mother had been less enthused at the idea of Stella spending the holidays in Canada, but she could hardly argue about the benefit this could have on Stella's career.

The dilemma of her apparent abandonment here at the airport shook her confidence though. If her mom ever found out, she'd never let Stella hear the end of it. Stella could hear the screeches her mother would have made, reminding Stella that if she'd stayed in the limelight a bit more, no one would ever forget her at an airport again.

Pushing an unruly lock of hair away from her face, Stella considered the options and struggled to regain some control. She could snag a taxi and cart all of her luggage along for the ride while she went to St. Matthew's and tried to find the elusive Dr. Cook, or she could wait and hope he hadn't forgotten her entirely.

Was there a currency exchange in this airport? There should be, right? She wouldn't be able to pay for the taxi without the proper currency. That should have been on her list of things to take care of before her flight. *Bit late for that now.*

No notifications on her phone meant no reply to the sent email. Oh, she didn't like this. Her teeth worried her lower lip while she mulled over her alternatives.

"Dr. Allen?" a man called from her left.

She turned that direction but the only person looking her way was a father with a small child in his arms. If she weren't looking for someone else, he wouldn't be a bad one to rest her eyes on for a bit. With a wistful sigh, her gaze flicked away from the small family to search for the source of her name.

A tall, athletic frame blocked her view as the man carrying the little boy stopped directly in front of her. His short brown hair looked like he'd been running his hands through it, but somehow the disheveled aspect of his appearance didn't detract from his appeal at all. Stella's heart raced as they made eye contact.

"Are you Dr. Stella Allen?" Apparently, he *had* been the one calling her name and she'd been too quick to dismiss him. Admittedly, she'd been expecting a doctor, not someone on daddy duty.

"Yes, I'm Stella Allen." She flashed him a

smile. Had Dr. Cook had an emergent case show up and needed to find someone to pick her up last-minute? Maybe options were slim this evening. “And you are?”

“Dr. Aiden Cook. We’ve been exchanging emails.” His curt tone turned her genuine smile into the practiced fake she’d perfected over years for the cameras.

Straightening her spine, she narrowed her eyes at him. “I assumed that, given the late time, and the presence of a child, Dr. Cook must have had an emergency and sent you in his stead.”

Her barb struck home and a small muscle in his jaw twitched.

“I had…” He trailed off, readjusting his hold on the child. “I was nearly here when the day care called in a panic. Jamie was upset and needed me immediately. I apologize for my lateness and any inconvenience it might have caused you.”

The apology didn’t ring quite true. His words professed apology, but there was a hardness in his brown eyes that didn’t agree with the soft words. Somehow, she instinctively knew that he’d leave her standing alone again if little

Jamie needed something in the future and she found it hard to fault him for that. Would her own parents have put her first had they been in Dr. Cook's situation? Would they have inconvenienced a professional contact to soothe their upset child? The answer she arrived at was disheartening.

"You could have let me know," she murmured.

"I might have, if I had remembered to get your number." His deep voice still held only the slightest hint of apology. "Are you ready to go then?"

"I am. I've already collected from baggage claim."

He glanced at the pile of luggage at her feet. "Did you bring everything you own? It is a two-month stay, not a permanent move after all."

Who did this guy think he was?

A huff of disbelief escaped her as she followed his gaze to her belongings. She'd brought with her two large suitcases, a carry-on and her admittedly large purse. It was hardly a ridiculous amount given that she was scheduled to spend nearly two months in Toronto.

"I assure you that I've carried nothing unnecessary across the Atlantic Ocean simply for the back pain. Not that it is truly your business, but in addition to clothing for both work and home, I have my computer equipment and materials for my presentation. Believe me when I say that I brought nothing that wasn't an absolute requirement. I hardly overpacked."

The hint of an eye roll he gave when she mentioned her show irritated her even more. The theme of this particular film project had been one she'd been hoping to do since her residency. It had taken her years to convince her contacts to take it on, and even longer to convince a hospital to be open to the project. Now that she'd been given the go-ahead, she was not going to let some grumpy ER doctor ruin the excitement for her.

"Do you have a problem with the fact that I will be filming a television special about the hardworking men and women in and around the emergency department of St. Matthew's? Because I assure you, it was cleared by people well above your pay grade."

His eyes hardened. "Keep your cameras off

me and we will have no problem. I have no desire to be on screen at any time."

"Noted." The sooner she could get away from this man, the better. So much for the warm Canadian welcome she'd been expecting! Although, of all people, Stella should know that what was shown on television and in the media was not always accurate.

"Where is your camera crew?" He growled the question out so low it sounded like a threat.

"Following a bit behind, I'm afraid. It's just me today." She wasn't sure how long the film crew would be delayed, but with her participation in The Kensington Project she'd have plenty to keep her busy. Too much, perhaps, given that she'd be practically performing two full-time jobs through Christmas.

"Well, they'll need to make their own arrangements to get from the airport to their lodging and the hospital. I'm not a rideshare driver."

"Good thing as the poor reviews would keep you from getting fares." She glared at him in frustration. She wanted to get to her rental, take a nice hot shower and hopefully get some sleep, not continue to stand in the airport and banter with a man who clearly wanted to rid himself of her presence. Slipping the strap to her carry-on over her shoulder, she tilted her chin toward the exit. "Could you please show me to where I'll be staying? It's been a rather long day for me."

As she reached for her luggage, his hand settled over hers on one of the handles. Enough sparks flew between them to light up the city of Toronto for the rest of the evening. She recoiled like she'd been burned.

Well, sparks or not, nothing would be happening there. Aiden had a family, and her last relationship had stalled when she'd admitted that she wasn't ready to be a mum. Oliver had wanted to marry quickly and have their first child immediately. Things had ended rather abruptly when she'd confessed that she wasn't sure she ever wanted children.

Toronto held a job for her, not the promise of romance. Although, Aiden was rather easy on the eyes and the mere touch of his hand on hers made her feel things she hadn't felt in quite some time. She rubbed her hand against the fabric of her jacket and wished she could erase the warmth of his touch.

He's off-limits, Stella. Pull yourself together.

Even if she were looking for a bit of fun while she was there—which she was not—it would not be with someone at St. Matthew's Hospital. She was a professional and she couldn't risk the reputation of The Kensington Project, or the Royal Kensington Hospital where she'd be returning to her position in the orthopedic department at the start of the New Year.

"Would you like me to get your bag?" he asked gruffly.

Nodding, she waved at the bag closest to him. "Thank you."

Had the touch affected him the way it had her? She spared a glance in his direction. He was staring at her, his expression unreadable, but there was a twinkle in his brown eyes that made her think he'd experienced something similar.

Aiden balanced Jamie on his hip with his left arm and led Dr. Allen out of the airport while pulling her rather heavy suitcase with his right. Other than a few directional cues, they walked silently into the parking garage. They'd clearly gotten off on the wrong foot, but he didn't have the time or the inclination to make nice with a high-maintenance TV star who enjoyed the limelight.

Aiden didn't even like having his picture taken.

She'd grown up in front of the camera, so he doubted she had any shyness about having a lens aimed at her. He'd watched a good number of clips of her online. It had been simply research, he'd told himself. Just a way of learning what the person was like who he'd be working with day in and day out for the next two months.

Except, he'd found himself watching everything he could find about her, from the childhood show to the solo college endeavor. But it was the more recent clips as resident doctor on a British morning show that held him captive, lulled by the sound of her voice. Her accented speech soothed edges he hadn't known needed soothing. It didn't hurt that she was easy on the eyes.

Not his normal type though.

He glanced down at Jamie and his jaw tightened. Jamie's mother had been exactly his type. Tall and blond, with legs for days. For the one night, he'd been what she was looking for, as well. He'd gone into their evening together with the expectation that he'd never see her again. He hadn't expected a son as a result of that one-night stand either.

Maybe curvy brunettes were more his type now, because he couldn't take his eyes off Stella. The chemistry between them had nearly blown him away. If he hadn't had Jamie to serve as a buffer between them, that bit of argument they'd had in the airport might have gone nuclear. And he didn't just mean in anger. There was definitely a strong undercurrent of interest floating between them.

He needed to ignore it, but he certainly hadn't missed it.

"The information I was given said that a flat had been secured for me near St. Matthew's?"

"Yes." The small one-bedroom had been a temporary home to a variety of specialists and clinicians. Aiden himself had helped at least two other doctors get settled there for short-term assignments at St. Matthew's.

"The hospital keeps an apartment on lease at a mid-rise building just a block and a half south of St. Matthew's for visiting surgeons and lecturers. There's a shopping center a few blocks the other direction. It's well-placed if you prefer not to have a vehicle while you're here."

He was grateful for the distraction from the turn his thoughts had taken. Replaying those memories wouldn't change the reality and he didn't need to go down that road again. Britney had made her choice, and it wasn't being a mother to Jamie. He had sole physical custody, but until he could be one-hundred-percent certain that Britney wasn't going to reappear and mess things up, he couldn't take any chances. If Britney resurfaced, it could impact the progress Jamie had made. Jamie's needs had to be his number-one priority. Aiden just couldn't let himself forget the pain an actress could cause when she moved on to the next project.

He stopped next to his SUV and fished his keys out of his pocket. Turning off the alarm, he unlocked the doors. He moved to the side of the vehicle, explaining his actions as he went. "I'm just going to get Jamie buckled in and then I'll help you load the suitcases in the back."

Carefully, he buckled his son into the car seat already strapped into the backseat. "There you go, little guy," he said, making some funny faces at his son while he adjusted the straps.

When he closed the back door and turned back to Dr. Allen, she was giving him a softly indulgent smile. When their eyes met though, her expression hardened.

Good. She didn't need to be giving him sweet little smiles. They were barely colleagues. He certainly didn't need her to get the impression that he wanted to be more. He barely had time to himself, and he wouldn't be wasting any of his precious moments away from the hospital on another woman with an eye for showbiz. Stella Allen was only in Toronto temporarily, and he'd do well to remember that, even if she did evoke desires in him that he hadn't experienced in a while.

He popped the hatch and put her two suitcases inside. "Do you want to put your carry-on back here or hold on to it?"

She put the bag next to her suitcases without

another word. She stalked around to the driver's door carrying only her purse.

He stood by the end of the SUV and waited for her to realize her mistake.

She opened the door and the color drained from her face. "You lot drive on the right," she mumbled, coming back his direction.

"Yes, we do." He bit back a smile. Working with the woman was going to be entertaining, if nothing else.

"Do not laugh at me," she practically growled.

He chuckled. "Don't make it so easy."

She crossed her arms and rose up to her full height, all of maybe five foot six. Her green eyes flashed her displeasure. The look in her eyes said that she'd kill him and have him six feet under before his next laugh.

It only served to make her more intriguing. In fact, if his son hadn't been with them, he'd have been tempted to soothe her fraying temper with a little wine. Maybe after that, he could take her to her new apartment and see exactly how her curves fit in his arms.

No, he needed to keep it professional. He needed to keep his distance. Even if her lips begged to be kissed and his hands ached to feel the softness of her skin.

"You are quite rude," she said. He almost expected her to stomp her foot.

"I apologize," he said, with little sincerity. She'd amused him. He wouldn't really apologize for that. His words were meant to soothe her scuffed ego, because if her temper got any hotter, steam might come out her ears. It was tempting to push her until she blew up, just to see if he could goad her into kissing him.

Opening her mouth as if to speak, she second-guessed herself and simply shook her head. She walked around him and got into the passenger seat.

Climbing behind the wheel, he glanced over at her. "Since it's getting late, I thought I would let you settle in at the apartment and then take you over to the hospital for the grand tour in the morning?"

"That's probably best. I doubt you want to cart your son through the hospital. Too many ickies he could acquire."

He lifted an eyebrow slowly. Her unexpected word choice required a comment. *"Ickies?"*

Rolling her eyes, she waved a hand in frustration. "Would you prefer I get technical? We are speaking of a toddler. Forgive me for being a bit casual."

With a shrug, he said, "Point taken."

Carefully, he backed out of the parking space and turned the vehicle toward the exit. The silence of the car quickly became a nuisance. Soon, he found himself making small talk. And he loathed small talk.

"Have you ever been to Toronto?" he asked.

"First time." She scanned the darkened streets as they drove.

"Summer would have been a better time to visit."

A deep sigh escaped her. "I know. One of my colleagues is arriving in Jamaica as we speak. Lucky thing. Although, if I'd been assigned there, it would have been hard to convince my mum that she and my dad shouldn't follow for a family holiday. So, Toronto is better."

"I'm sensing there's a story there." He'd seen her parents in some of her childhood shows when he'd researched her. They'd seemed caring, but her mother had come across as a little overbearing.

"We don't know each other nearly well enough for me to spill secrets that classified."

He snorted. "We don't know each other at all."

"Half my life has been on camera." Her deep sigh filled the car. "The few secrets I have I like to keep close."

"Yeah, I…uh…saw that you'd been part of a few television shows."

That fact alone was enough for him to avoid an entanglement with Stella. After Britney, he'd never get involved with another actress. He was still smoking from the burns she'd set ablaze in his life. Anyone who made their living in front of the camera was no one he wanted to get entangled with. Some lessons took the first time and didn't have to be learned again.

"So, you Googled me?" she asked, and he could hear the mirth in her voice. He imagined her eyes would be twinkling as well if he looked her direction.

He opened his mouth to make a sarcastic reply, but stopped himself. Some topics just weren't worth commenting on. Instead, Aiden kept his eyes firmly on the pavement in front of him. The temperatures had dropped below freezing and he didn't want to risk an accident just to see if he was right about her eyes sparkling in amusement.

CHAPTER THREE

AIDEN MADE THE VEHICLE feel microscopic. His broad shoulders took up more than his share of space in the front, and more than that, he had a larger-than-life presence without even trying.

Stella really tried not to look at him. She kept her eyes firmly on the scenery outside the window—at least what scenery was illuminated by streetlamps. They drove by building after building, but very little could be seen in the darkness of the evening.

"If you'd been on time, perhaps I could have actually seen some of the sights," she jabbed at him, not so subtly. Something about him had turned off her politeness and made her want to provoke him, and she couldn't quite pinpoint the why. Maybe that he was late? Maybe that he'd laughed at her for going round the wrong side of the car? Maybe that he made her want things she couldn't have? "Couldn't your wife have picked up the child?"

"His name is Jamie." The force behind his words drew her gaze. Hands gripping the wheel tightly, he spoke through clenched teeth, "And I'm not married."

"His mother, then."

"Not. An. Option." His tone grew darker, his words laced with an unvoiced finality, marking the conversation over and unavailable for further discussion.

Curiosity filled her. There was a story hidden in Aiden's reaction. Stealing glances in his direction, she noted the stiffness in his limbs, the way his hand gripping the steering wheel with unnecessary pressure and most of all, the "done with it all" look on his face. For a second, she thought she heard his teeth grinding together.

Not grief, then. Hmm.

Anger?

Definitely anger. The realization only made her more interested in finding out what had happened to wee Jamie's mum. But she'd pushed her luck with the man next to her too much already that night so she'd have to fish for answers later. She worried her lower lip with her teeth as she considered him.

Running a quick recap in her head, she recalled what she knew about Dr. Aiden Cook. It was so very little. He worked in the emergency department at St. Matthew's where she was about to spend the next two months. And he was apparently a single dad to an adorable little tot.

A devoted dad, came the thought, unbidden. A sexy, devoted dad.

No, no, no.

She gave herself a bit of a mental shake. She didn't date dads at home, so she certainly wouldn't start in Canada. She'd decided years ago that children weren't in the cards for her. Why was the idea of dating Aiden Cook even a thought? She closed her eyes tight in frustration. This man was getting far too much of her thoughts and attention.

Her presence in Toronto was for two reasons, and two reasons alone—to present her highly innovative orthopedic surgery technique and film her holiday special. Her career was finally on the trajectory that she herself wanted and she wasn't going to let the shadows lurking in a pair of velvety brown eyes distract her from that path. She inhaled deeply, hoping to cement her resolve, and came away with a lungful of very masculine-scented air.

Of course he had to smell delicious.

The off-limits fellows always did, didn't they?

Aiden broke the silence with a surprise question. "What did your boyfriend think of you leaving him behind to come to Canada?"

The query caught her off guard. It wasn't something she'd expected him to ask. It piqued her curiosity. He must've noticed the sparks between them too then.

"I don't have a boyfriend," she answered softly.

"Imagine that." Aiden snorted. "Did you run him off too with your inability to keep your nose out of private details?"

"I beg your pardon!" Her mouth gaped while she tried to wrap her head around the rudeness of the man. How dare he make such assumptions about her! Blood boiling at the conjectures, the beginning of a tension headache tightened her frame. This man might drive her right over the edge into full-blown insanity.

Lord knows her mother had come close more than a few times.

"We're here. I'll help you get your bags upstairs and then pick you up in the morning to go over to the hospital." He turned the SUV into an underground garage. "I'd say you could find your own way tomorrow, but sadly I've been tasked with assisting you while you are here."

"Believe me when I say that I have as little interest in spending time with you as you have in spending time with me." Muscles tensed, Stella waited for him to say something else.

Parking the SUV in a space near the elevator, Aiden said nothing though. She looked his way but he never so much as flicked his eyes toward her a single time. He turned the engine off and hit a button to open the back hatch. The warmth of the cabin disappeared in the span of a blink, replaced with wintry cold.

Stella suppressed a shiver before stepping out of the vehicle. At least the cold was calming the white-hot temper that Aiden ignited. She moved to the back and reached in for her bags only to once again find her hand covered by one of Aiden's.

"It seems our hands like each other even if we can't stand one another," she muttered.

"Hmph." He grunted as he lifted her heaviest bit of luggage out of the SUV. "Maybe you just need to pay more attention to what you're doing."

It wasn't a question. No, Aiden's words could only be described as a demand. It wasn't a statement, but an *order.*

Stella bristled. Who did he think he was? She would not be bossed around by some puffed-up egotistical emergency doctor. Eyes narrowing, she put her hands on her hips. "And perhaps you might listen to yourself there as both times now *your* hand has gotten to the bag *after* mine. Seems you are the one not as aware as he should be of his surroundings."

A noise reminiscent of a growl came from Aiden. "Now, listen here—"

Stella shook her head. "No. You listen. This whole caveman vibe you have might work for some women, but I assure you, it does not work on me. You have a problem with me, then come to me with a calm discussion. Otherwise, keep your anger out of my way. I have a job to do and I won't allow your Neanderthal behavior to derail me."

He moved closer and her breath caught. Heart thudding behind her ribs at a painful pace, she swallowed hard but held her ground. She'd dealt with bullies before and she wouldn't be starting off a new position in fear of one.

Slowly, his hand came up toward her face. Her eyes locked on his, trying to read him, to gauge if she was in real danger. She stood her ground as he merely brushed his fingers along her jawline.

The soft touch of his fingertips against her sensitive skin made her heart pound in her chest. She reached out and grabbed the side of the car to ground herself. The simple graze packed a powerful punch. The gentleness behind his touch and the look in his eyes told her she was safe physically, but Aiden Cook was a dangerous man—to her heart and soul.

"Got it." His words were soft, nearly inaudible, but she had no trouble comprehending his meaning.

Figuring out the puzzle that Aiden Cook presented though?

That was going to be the challenge.

* * *

Aiden grabbed Stella's bags from the back of his vehicle and set them roughly at his feet. What was he thinking touching her like that? The woman infuriated him. He shouldn't be thinking about kissing her!

He slammed the lid to the hatch and stomped around her and her pile of luggage to get Jamie out of his car seat.

Keeping his voice even and calm, he spoke to his son. "Hey, kiddo, we need to go inside for just a minute to help Dr. Allen find her apartment, okay?"

Jamie nodded solemnly as Aiden unbuckled him. Everything the little guy did was solemn. He was quiet unless spoken to. Even in play he made far less noise than most of the two-year-olds Aiden had seen in his life. Nothing broke through the protective wall that Jamie had erected around his heart. At only two, he had already faced losses that most people couldn't understand.

Hopefully, one day soon, Jamie would see that Aiden would never abandon him though. Hopefully, Jamie would know just how much he was loved. Maybe then he would grace them with a smile or a laugh. Until then, Aiden would continue to spend every moment he could with his son, and pray that it was enough.

"Jamie walk?" his soft voice made Aiden's heart swell. The first month Jamie had lived with him, the child hadn't uttered a word. Trauma from his mother's abandonment was what the doctors had said. Even now, Jamie only spoke occasionally. Aiden had sadly related all too well to the feeling of abandonment. Hopefully, his son was young enough that it wouldn't carry over through adulthood for him like it had for Aiden who'd spent several years in foster care after his own birth mother had left him behind.

"If you hold my hand," Aiden said in reply.

Jamie nodded and held a mittened hand up for Aiden to clasp.

"Is he always so well-behaved?" Stella asked.

"Yes." His curt reply would hopefully stave off further questions. Jamie didn't like when anyone talked about him and even a simple conversation would have the boy withdrawing even more.

"Hmm..." She looked like she wanted to say

something else but thankfully got the message when Aiden shook his head quickly.

"The apartment is on the fourth floor." He gestured toward the bigger piece of luggage that they both seemed to go for first each time. "May I?"

She waved a hand at him. "Of course, thank you."

He walked slowly toward the elevator so that Jamie didn't have to run. Not that the little guy would complain, but Aiden did his best to make sure his son was comfortable when he could. It was hard when the kid just wouldn't say when something bothered him.

Stella crouched down when they reached the elevator and asked, "Do you want to push the button? I always loved the lift buttons when I was small."

Jamie moved back behind Aiden's leg, peering around at Stella cautiously.

"Is that a no?" she tried again, smiling softly at him. "Last chance," she said, holding her hand over the still dark button.

Jamie tentatively reached a hand, but halted, looking up to Aiden for permission.

"You can push it—go ahead."

Cautiously, Jamie took a step out from behind Aiden and reached out. He couldn't quite reach. He took one more step, and again tried to reach.

Stella eased back.

Still firmly gripping Aiden's hand with his much smaller one, Jamie finally reached over and pushed the button. When the light lit up he made the tiniest of squeals.

Aiden had to fight back a few tears of joy. That was the closest thing he'd heard to a laugh from his son since the day Jamie had come into his life nine months ago. He wanted to thank Stella for it, but at the same time there was a tiny sliver of hurt that she'd managed to pull a response from Jamie that he hadn't yet.

"Good job!" Stella encouraged.

Her enthusiastic words sent Jamie back into hiding mode though, and he ducked back behind Aiden. And clearly the moment was over. Jamie tugged at his hand. When he looked down, Jamie held up his arms, asking to be picked up.

Lifting his son into his arms, he let the boy snuggle in how he liked and then kissed the top of his head. Who knew he'd like being a father so much? Honestly, he'd never planned to have kids. Now he couldn't imagine a life without his son in it. He just wished Jamie were happier.

The elevator doors opened and they moved inside without another word. Stella hit the button for the fourth floor silently. She must have realized Jamie wasn't interested in pushing another button.

"Four-o-two," he directed when they reached the correct floor.

When they reached the door, he fished through his pockets for the keys. He handed them over to Stella to let her handle the lock. Juggling keys and a toddler was something he was still learning to do.

Stella walked in and he could see the approval on her face as she took in the apartment. It was small, but well-appointed. His last apartment had been similar. It was a good fit for a single person.

Aiden rolled the suitcase to a spot where it would be out of the way. He looked at Stella and said, "I wasn't sure what foods you normally eat, but I did stock the kitchen with a small variety of things. Soups, pastas, mostly shelf-stable things. Hopefully, you'll find something to tide you over until you can do your own shopping."

"I'm not a fussy eater, so I'm sure whatever you've provided will be acceptable." Stella shrugged out of her coat and hung it on a hook on the wall. "I do appreciate it."

"Of course." He turned to go.

"Dr. Cook?"

"Aiden, please," he said.

"I want to apologize. It seems we've gotten off on a bit of the wrong foot. We're meant to be working together for the next several weeks, and I would so like that to be on polite terms at the least."

He nodded. "I think we both crossed a line tonight. You must be exhausted from your journey, and my evening got sidetracked. That likely put us both on edge and made us snappier than usual. So, I also apologize for my behavior."

"Well, here's to a fresh start then," Stella said with a smile that didn't quite reach her eyes. She held a hand out to him. "Should we shake on it?"

After the sparks that had flown each time

they'd accidentally touched, Aiden was hesitant to put his skin to hers voluntarily. But it would be rude to ignore her outstretched hand.

"To fresh starts," he said, clasping her hand with his.

The early sparks blazed up into an inferno of awareness. He pulled his hand away as quickly as was polite and flexed it a few times, trying to rid himself of the way her touch made him feel. He didn't have room in his life for a woman right now, temporarily or otherwise.

With a curt "Good night," Aiden quickly left, carrying Jamie in his arms.

When the elevator doors closed, shutting away his view of the door to Stella's apartment, he released a deep breath. "Jamie, buddy, don't grow up. Women are bewildering creatures that a man can't decide if he wants to kiss or run from."

Jamie gave him a confused look.

"You'll understand when you're older." His brow furrowed. "Maybe."

CHAPTER FOUR

STELLA DRESSED CAREFULLY for her first day at St. Matthew's Hospital. The brief packet of information she'd received hadn't mentioned the dress code preferred by the administration, but she couldn't be faulted for a crisp business suit with tasteful and comfortable flats. She did slip a scrub uniform and a pair of sneakers into her bag, in case they did prefer her to wear scrubs.

But imagine if she arrived in her pink scrubs to find that surgeons were expected to be in business dress unless they were operating that day? How would anyone take her seriously if she couldn't properly follow a dress code?

No, the charcoal suit was the sensible, safe choice until she learned her way around here. Making a good first impression meant everything. After the rocky beginning with Dr. Cook last night, she needed to start off on the right track at St. Matthew's more than ever.

She applied a minimal amount of makeup—just enough to hide the fact that only two days ago she'd been six time zones away—and styled her dark bob simply. Given that she'd soon be digging deeply into everyone's thoughts and feelings as part of the television special she'd be filming, she wanted to look professional, but approachable. Years spent in front of the camera had taught her to appear unassuming and collected if she wanted genuine responses.

Yet she also wanted to look her best for when she next saw Aiden. Just the idea of seeing him again immediately made her heart beat erratically, like a schoolgirl with a crush. She pursed her lips in frustration. In the mirror, her reflection frowned back at her while her cheeks pinked up.

She took in a deep breath and calmed herself. Dr. Aiden Cook's looks didn't matter to her, even if he was one of the most striking men she'd ever been near. And the chemistry that sparked up between them was no insignificant matter, but he was a grumpy single father and she was not motherhood material.

Her own mother had hardly set a shining example of what it meant to be a proper mum. Oh, Debra Allen had fawned over her, particularly once she'd had Stella's IQ tested and the results came in showing her to be a genius. Stella believed that her mother's actions were based on love—after all, she frequently referred to Stella as her miracle baby—but she was quite selfish and never put Stella first. Was that what parental love was meant to be like? Her mum had never stopped once to consider whether the on-screen life they were forcing her into was what Stella really wanted.

Sure, it had given Stella a tidy little nest egg, but there'd never been any normalcy. Stella's first kiss had been caught on camera. The tabloids knew when she'd been dumped, sometimes before she did. All she'd ever wanted was a normal life.

She was still musing over why she'd stayed in the television business after she'd become an adult when a knock on the door drew her back to her present reality.

As she swung it open, she had to tamp down her excitement to see Aiden.

Pull yourself together, Stella!

"Good morning, Dr. Allen, are you ready

to head over to the hospital?" His brown hair shone in the morning light pouring in from the large window in the hallway. It also helped to emphasize just how well-built he was. His broad shoulders filled the open doorway. Even in scrubs, she could tell that Dr. Cook was quite fit.

"Stella, please," she said as she pulled her coat on, hoping it didn't muss her suit too much. The temperatures here were just too low to leave it behind though. Still, if Dr. Cook didn't stop looking at her like that, she might not need any clothes to stay warm.

How could a mere glance from him make her feel so heated? With Oliver, her last boyfriend, she had never had such chemistry. In fact, most of her past experiences had left her cold and uncertain as to why romance was so important to others.

"Stella, then," he said.

She couldn't quite suppress the shudder that the sound of her name on his lips wrought on her senses. His deep voice seemed made to utter her name. She'd always hated her name, thinking it too old-fashioned and stuffy, but hearing those two syllables roll off Aiden's tongue might change her mind.

"I hope you got some rest?" He raised a single eyebrow at her. From the twinkle in his eyes, he'd not missed her unwanted reaction to him. Unintentionally, she'd fluffed his ego.

Great.

Swallowing hard, she chose to ignore the unspoken query and focus solely on what he'd asked verbally. "Indeed, the furnishings are lovely. Once I fully adjust to the time difference, I think I'll be quite comfortable."

"Do you need any of your camera equipment today?" He nodded toward the video equipment she'd laid out on the table.

"Not today. Meetings with the medical director and the head of orthopedics today. And I'm to get my ID badge and stop in at human resources." Stella continued the conversation as she locked the door to the apartment. "Additionally, I thought it best to introduce myself and settle in a touch before pointing a camera at anyone. Hardly the way to make friends, you see. And I won't be doing the bulk of the filming, as that will be left to the film crew once they get here. I'll only be doing some more informal, intimate conversation-type shots."

"If you do bring it, don't point it at me."

His words held a gruffness that she'd started to associate with him, particularly when the subject of her television show came up. She wasn't quite sure if it came as a result of a fear of cameras or a personal vendetta toward show business, but it was hardly something she could ignore. Filming was a priority and it would be hard to get enough material shot without ever catching him on camera when he was her liaison with the hospital.

"At all?"

He glared at her as she stepped into the elevator next to him. "I'd really rather you didn't."

"You have the type of looks that will draw female viewers though." She tried a little flattery, mostly to see if she was correct in her guess at how he would respond.

"Pass." Aiden snorted. His tone made his annoyance clear even within that single syllable.

Interesting. He'd responded quite as she'd expected. Knowing he was a single parent, she had considered that he might not want the likely aftereffects that his participation on the show might bring. Still, perhaps he might be a little lonely.

"You might enjoy the attention that it brings you." She continued to push him, curious to see if it was a hurdle he'd clear quickly once the initial protests had left his mind. She'd seen more than one shy person put their fears aside in hopes of finding a new love interest. Although, in her experience, men who looked like Aiden would have little trouble drawing attention.

He shook his head. "Doubtful."

"One day, I will get the story from you as to why you are so camera shy."

"How do you know there's a story?" The gruffness returned to his voice. "You don't know me."

Stella shrugged and affected a mysterious air. At least she hoped that's how she looked. "If it was simply that you hated having your portrait taken, you'd have said. My years of experience have taught me that this level of avoidance is more than that. But perhaps we don't know each other well enough for you to share yet."

"Hmph." His frustrated noise confirmed that suspicion, as well.

If she wanted to get to the bottom of his reluctance, she'd have to earn a bit of his trust first. Somehow, she knew Aiden wouldn't trust easily though. What had caused his trust issues? She could see them as easily as she could his problem with being on camera.

Jamie's mother, maybe?

"I have zero interest in being a part of your program." Maybe if he spelled it out specifically, word for word, she'd catch on.

"So, you don't want to find love?" This woman was persistent. Aiden struggled not to snap when she kept pushing him to be on camera. He had already told her he wasn't interested. How many ways did he need to say it? Did she require it in writing?

"No more than I want to be set on fire."

"Everyone deserves love, Aiden."

"So, you've met your soul mate then? The man you intend to live your life with, from now to eternity?"

"We weren't speaking of me." Her cheeks tinted pink when the focus of the conversation shifted to her. The color only served to highlight her beauty.

Aiden had to pull his gaze away from her. It took effort, but he needed to concentrate on the road. "I'm not looking for a soul mate, or a playmate, or any other sort of mate at this point in my life."

Why had he just confessed that? He normally played his cards close to the vest. He didn't share details of his life with virtual strangers.

"But..."

"No buts, Stella. I'm okay as I am."

He couldn't say he was happy. *Content* was even a stretch. But right now, Jamie was the only person he could think of. Maybe once Jamie was more settled and less fragile, maybe then he could consider dating again.

"Your ex did a real number on you, didn't she?"

Aiden's hands clenched around the steering wheel. "Are you willing to tell me all about your exes then?"

"Hardly."

"Then perhaps keep your questioning to yourself." He could feel his blood pressure rising as thoughts of Britney filled his mind. Had his ex done a number on him? Oh, yeah, she had, but indirectly. She hadn't broken his heart by stepping out on him with another man. She hadn't stolen his money and disappeared. No, what she'd done was much worse. She'd hurt Aiden by neglecting their son, by keeping their son from him. That was not a conversation he was willing to have with a so-called doctor more concerned with filming a television show than with medicine.

Silence filled the car as they continued their short commute.

"There's the main entrance that you'll want to use if you're walking to work," Aiden said gruffly, gesturing as they passed by the front of the hospital. "Employee parking garage is just around the next corner."

Stella murmured a thanks but kept quiet otherwise.

"Where are you supposed to be this morning?" he asked as he pulled into his parking space. They constantly rubbed each other the wrong way, but he couldn't in good conscience leave her with no direction.

"I'm to meet Dr. Stone first thing. Not quite sure beyond that."

He couldn't help but notice that Stella appeared a little nervous. Hmm… So she didn't have nerves of steel after all. Interesting. "First day jitters?"

"I'll be fine," she said, giving him a thousand-watt smile that didn't quite reach her eyes.

"Let me show you to the admin wing before I head down to the ED."

He guided her through the employee entrance without touching her. Touching her had proven to be a bad idea. Every single time he did, it made him think about things and want things that he just couldn't have.

CHAPTER FIVE

NO MATTER HOW old you were, the first week at a new job was never easy. The medical director at St Matthew's Hospital had a brusque, no-nonsense demeanor that reminded Stella of the chief executive at her home hospital.

Stella had spent her entire first day with Dr. Stone going over the expectations for Stella's stay in Canada. There were plans for a regular lecture series so that she might share her technique with as many doctors as possible from St. Matthew's and the surrounding hospitals via prerecorded videos. Surgical privileges were extended for Stella if a patient presented who was a candidate for said technique with the understanding that there could be an audience who might view the surgery firsthand.

And, of course, there was discussion on how she might best highlight St. Matthew's for the television program. Dr. Stone had very strong opinions on how she wanted her hospital presented. Stella had given every reassurance that she'd be respectful of St. Matthew's well-earned reputation.

Day two had begun with a quick tour of the facility. So quick that Stella wasn't able to get her bearings at all. Given that it was her specialty, Stella was most interested in the orthopedic floor, but Dr. Stone wanted to keep moving. With a lingering glance, she followed the medical director away from orthopedics. She'd have to explore her temporary workplace more closely later. They walked briskly through the emergency department where Stella had to bite back her disappointment when she didn't catch so much as a glimpse of Aiden. Dr. Stone left her in the human resources department so that she could fill out some paperwork and get an ID badge made.

Stella left the HR offices hours later feeling rather like they'd scraped her bare and stolen part of her soul with all the forms she'd had to fill out. The picture on her newly laminated ID badge was her worst *ever* work picture and she'd begged the clerk to take another. The man had refused and even had a glimmer of joy in his eyes when he denied her request. Miserable toad must have had a bad morning to gain so much pleasure from causing others pain. At least she only had to carry this monstrosity of an identification card for two months.

Her week didn't get any better when her third day at St. Matthew's began with a few wrong turns that led her into the depths of the hospital. All of the corridors looked the same and the farther she walked, the less she recalled having seen before. When she somehow made a complete circle and ended up taking a second stroll past the same information desk, she had to admit defeat.

"Pardon me?" she asked the older gentleman at the desk.

"Guessing you must be lost," he said, with a raised eyebrow. Amusement lined his weathered face. "You just went by here a few minutes ago."

"I am." She admitted defeat. "Could you point me in the direction of orthopedics? I'm afraid I've gotten turned round and can't seem to find my way."

His already furrowed brow wrinkled farther.

"Normally don't get asked that one. Most just ask directions to Emergency."

"Well, can you give me directions to the emergency department then? I can make my way from there."

Aiden was working in the ED and he'd surely point the way for her. Her heart rate sped up at the thought of seeing him again, and she tried her best to put that attraction out of her mind.

Why did she have to have a thing for the grumpy guy?

She'd been teased for her taste in men before. For some undeterminable reason, Stella always gravitated toward the guys who verged on being total assholes. In the movies, she loved when the gruff loner fell head over heels for the heroine and was soft only for his woman.

Snarky comments and curt tones were like catnip to Stella. And when they combined with the athletic build and classic good looks in a man like Aiden, well, Stella was going to have to watch herself around him.

It helped a bit that Aiden had made it clear he wasn't interested in her or anything she stood for. He would at least want to keep the distance, even if she strayed across the invisible boundary between them. Despite his apology after their short car ride to the hospital on Monday, he wasn't her biggest fan. He hadn't sought her out at all since. Somehow, inexplicably, that made him more desirable. Her silly hormones had her reacting to a man she didn't even like. Who didn't like her. If she'd gone into psychology, perhaps she'd understand what that might say about her.

One thing she did know was why she was devoutly single. She always went for the wrong guys. Always.

After the way things had ended between her and Oliver, lessons should have been learned. The words coworker and brooding would be numbers one and two on a list of the types of men who should be avoided at all costs. Stella thought she'd learned, but this white-hot attraction to Aiden Cook made it glaringly obvious that her taste in men was still extremely questionable.

Shaking her head, Stella focused on the task at hand—finding the emergency department. When she rounded a corner, she let out a small sigh of relief.

Finally...

Walking up to the reception desk under a large sign that read Emergency, Stella asked, “Where might I find Dr. Cook?”

After looking her up and down, the nurse manning the desk said slowly, “If you’d like to give your name and take a seat, I can page him for you.”

Flashing her shiny new identification, Stella replied, “I’d rather you just aim me in his direction. I’m Dr. Stella Allen from The Kensington Project and Dr. Cook is my liaison here. I’ve only just arrived this week, so I’m still finding my way.”

“I’ll page him.” The nurse smiled the fakest smile.

Stella replied with a fake smile of her own. While she really didn’t want to get off on the wrong foot on her first day, she hated having to accept the brushoff. “I’ll just wait here then.”

“There’s seating just there.” The nurse waved vaguely to the right where several rows of seating formed a waiting area.

Stella held her position. “I’ll sit once you’ve paged him.”

This nurse appeared against the idea of Stella being anywhere near Aiden. He had implied that he didn't date, but the nurse in front of her didn't seem to have gotten the memo. Stella wasn't going to back down on this matter though. She'd accept him being paged over being sent in his direction, but she wouldn't sit until she saw or heard the nurse actually page him. That way she could be sure it was done now versus an hour from now.

Fake smile falling quickly from her face, the nurse puffed up and sent a glare in Stella's direction that might wither a lesser woman. But Stella had been raised by Debra Allen, the queen of hard looks, and was made of sterner stuff.

Stella's answering look was a genuine smile, because she'd won this round. "I'll wait."

The nurse made a noise that reminded Stella of a growl, but she picked up the phone. "Dr. Cook to the ED desk. Dr. Aiden Cook to the ED desk." Slamming the receiver down, she asked in a waspy tone, "Happy?"

"Very." Stella beamed at her. "Thank you. I do appreciate your assistance in this matter."

She stepped away before the nurse could say another word. Hopefully by ending on such a happy note, she hadn't completely burned the bridge with that particular nurse. She did have to spend the next two months here in Toronto and she couldn't afford to make enemies so early on.

Perched on the uncomfortable chair, Stella waited patiently for Aiden. As she sat there, she people watched. People watching had always been something she'd loved to do, even as a child. She loved to see the little interactions between coworkers and families; the interplay of nonverbal communications and verbal fascinated her. Psychology had been her initial focus, but then she had watched a documentary about orthopedic studies. From that moment on, ortho had become her passion. She'd gone through medical school with the singular ambition to become an orthopedic surgeon. Oh, she'd done the other rotations—emergency, internal medicine, obstetrics—but ortho had been her goal from day one.

Besides being a preferred pastime, people watching also let Stella look for potential subjects for her program. The sour-faced nurse at the desk was certainly not going on camera, unless her attitude drastically improved. A couple doctors strolled past, clearly enthralled with each other. Were they a couple? Adding in a segment on how the stresses of the job affected relationships could be interesting.

Stella dug through her purse for her phone to make a note of that idea before she forgot. The notes app on her phone got a lot of use while she was working on a program. Tapping out her thoughts, she suddenly felt rather than saw Aiden's arrival.

As she looked up, he strode up to the desk. The nurse looked at him with longing written all over her face, but he only barely shot the other woman a glance.

Stella had to squash some longing of her own when she and Aiden made eye contact. Swallowing hard, she rose to her feet as he moved in her direction.

"You paged?" His decidedly annoyed expression caused Stella to bristle defensively.

"She paged. I asked where I might find you." Stella wanted to clear that up. It wasn't her fault that the other woman took it upon herself to be a gatekeeper. "I'm sorry for interrupting your workday. I've had a tour of the hospital and yet wasn't sure I could find my way back to the orthopedic floor. I need to get your number, as well."

The nurse behind Aiden huffed.

Stella's lips turned up in the hint of a smile. She stepped a little closer to Aiden and placed her hand on his bare forearm. "I should have gotten your number when you dropped me off the other night, but I can only blame that slip on jet lag."

"What are you doing?" Aiden asked, his tone dark and low. His long lashes framed expressive brown eyes that were currently glittering with impatience.

"Testing a theory," Stella whispered back as she tilted her upper body slightly in Aiden's direction. Her experiment was wreaking havoc on her own senses, but she continued with her course of action, determined to prove her point.

Something slammed on the desk behind them and Aiden jumped at the sudden noise. His movement only served to bring him even closer to Stella.

"That nurse has a thing for you—did you know?" Stella allowed her fingers to trail softly over Aiden's skin. This might have started as a jab at the nurse, testing a theory that the nurse was attracted to Aiden, but now that her hand was on him, Stella didn't want to stop touching him. "If you are interested in her, now might be a good time for you to go express that interest."

He snorted. "Not in this lifetime."

"No?" She raised a single brow at him.

Shaking his head, Aiden doubled down on his rejection with a glance at the nurse behind him. "I don't date women from the hospital."

"That's just too bad, really," Stella murmured before she could stop herself. She had the same rule for herself, but she could see breaking it for a man like Aiden Cook. Some rules were just made to be broken, after all.

Aiden's eyes darkened in response to her words. He lowered his head and asked in a dangerously sexy tone, "Are you flirting with me, Dr. Allen?"

Stella's cheeks pinked up in response to his question. Her hand remained on his forearm, her lithe fingers trekking up and down his skin until it was all he could do not to yank her up against his chest and kiss her.

He had always made it a point not to date anyone from the hospital. He'd seen how badly workplace romances could go sideways early in his residency and he'd sworn he would never cross that line. Stella made him want to break that vow in a thousand different ways.

His plan had been to ignore her presence in his hospital and ED as much as possible, given that he'd been assigned to work with her. Knowing he'd be forced to interact with her, he'd accepted that he would have to see her. Yet he hadn't expected *this*.

How could he have expected that The Kensington Project visiting doctor would be the most infuriating woman—who also happened to be the sexiest woman—he'd ever been in contact with?

"You didn't answer my question," he prompted. He reached out and tipped her chin upward until she met his gaze. "Because it certainly seems like you are flirting."

She pulled away and took a step back, her cheeks darkening further. "Apologies. I..." she trailed off. What excuse had she been about to give him? The tidbit about testing to see if Nurse Rita was interested in him might have given her the impulse, but her own attraction was what kept that interaction going.

"If you're curious, I'm not seeing anyone," he said, while mentally kicking himself for volunteering that information. He really should keep his distance from the woman in front of him, but something about her pulled him in like gravity. His own attraction fueled that admission.

"Aww, geez, hold that thought, please. My memory card is full up and I need to switch it out right quick."

Aiden spun around.

A man stood a few feet away with a large camera on his shoulder. "Ah, there's the little bugger," he said as he pulled the small memory card out of the bottom of the messenger-style bag he had slung across his torso.

"I don't want to be on camera," Aiden growled.

"No?" The cameraman looked confused. "The chemistry between you two is priceless. It's the kind of stuff a director's dreams are made of."

"You shouldn't be filming me without my express permission." Aiden narrowed his eyes.

Stella inhaled a sharp breath behind him. He expected she'd wade in and argue once more that he should be flattered to be on camera and extoll the benefits of allowing a lens to invade his privacy.

He turned his glare on Stella. "And I thought you said your film crew wouldn't be here for a while?"

"I managed to finish my previous assignment a bit early," the videographer said, his tone so cheerful and happy that Aiden wanted to punch something.

"Dr. Cook to trauma one. Dr. Cook to trauma one," a nasally female voice called out over the PA system. He had to bite back a curse because the last thing he wanted right now was to run a trauma.

"To be continued?" Stella asked, a hopefulness in her tone that made him want to scream.

What was with these people? Why were they so annoyingly happy all the time? And why was she so gung ho about forcing him to be on camera? "There's nothing further to be said on the matter. I'm not interested."

He let the double entendre in that line stand between them. He wanted to make it crystal clear that he wasn't interested in being on camera or in being with her. Unless it was something physical only, he couldn't get involved.

Stella gave a brief nod, acknowledging silently that she'd caught his meaning. "Do you mind if I tag along on your trauma though? I'd like to see how you run things here. Get the lay of the land, so to speak."

When he shrugged, she fell into step next to him. The cameraman followed a few feet behind, but after Aiden glared at him, he lowered the camera.

Stella ignored the cameraman entirely and spoke as if they were alone. "I'd love to discuss my technique with you when you have a free moment. As an emergency doctor, you'll catch patients first so it would be helpful if you could give me a ring if someone fitting the criteria arrives in your care. I've videos, of course, but it's much more memorable if your surgeons here get a chance to practice it live. Recordings can only teach so much, after all."

"I'd agree with that." He scanned his ID badge to unlock the doors back into the emergency department. "And I'd love to hear more about this revolutionary technique of yours. It must be something for you to be sent halfway across the world to share it with us."

Aiden spared a glance for the cameraman, making sure the camera was still pointed down.

"Revolutionary might be a stretch," Stella continued, her tone modest and free of the boastful arrogance many surgeons assumed when discussing their work. Her eyes lit up with enthusiasm as she spoke though and that told him more than any of the videos he had watched about her medical skill. "I pioneered a technique that saves an average of an hour under anesthesia and it shortens the recovery time which leads to diminished muscle atrophy for patients with a broken pelvis. I have data to support that, if you are interested."

Maybe there was more substance to her than he'd initially given her credit for. He had basic knowledge of orthopedics, like all emergency room physicians, but he had a feeling that seeing Stella Allen operate would be a thing of beauty. While some of the details might go beyond him, he couldn't shake the desire to spend more time with her. The zest in her entire demeanor when she spoke of her technique inspired him to want to learn. She had a certain confidence when speaking of her work that was quite inspiring.

"I'm not a surgeon, but if you think I can help identify patients for you, then I'm interested in finding out more." Not just about her surgical advances, but about her, as well. Something inexplicable drove him to find out more about her, even if it was a bad idea.

They walked together into the trauma bay. He gave the cameraman a pointed look to keep his distance. Aiden pushed all thoughts of finding out more about Stella from his mind, and he turned his focus to the patient before him.

"Fill me in," he said as he gloved up.

"Elderly woman with a possible pelvic break sustained during a fall."

Kismet must have been at work since that very patient turned out to be ideal for Stella's technique. She allowed Aiden to work, not wanting to be a distraction while he stabilized the patient. It would have been great if he'd allowed Henry in, to film, but he'd been so opposed that she didn't want to push any further.

She'd have to bring it up when he was in a better mood.

Aiden was really quite thorough and his bedside manner surprised her. The gruff man she'd grown to expect was a real charmer with his patients. He put the older woman at ease within minutes and even got her to smile despite her pain. The gentle confidence he displayed with his patients showed her a different side of Aiden. What had made him so brusque?

"Dr. Allen, do you have anything to add?"

Stella glanced quickly at the list of tests and scans that Aiden had ordered for their patient, Mrs. Upton. He'd ordered nearly everything that she would have done, so she had little to add, although she did ask for a few more specific views to the requested scans.

A short while later, they were looking over the scans together. Aiden gave his interpretation and paused. Stella took that as her opportunity to speak up. "Your assessment that she has a fractured pelvis is spot-on. Might I show you where my skills come in?"

He nodded.

"See that break there," she said, pointing at the screen. "Traditionally, that would be a few pins here, here and there. Each taking time as the surgeon has to be super careful not to farther damage an already fragile bone."

"Right," Aiden said slowly. "I remember that much from my ortho rotation."

"I prefer to do things a bit differently," Stella continued. This was where she was in her element. In the operating room or talking about bones, Stella had full confidence. It was in the rest of her life that she had moments of uncertainty. "My technique came about because I had a patient whose bones were too brittle for the typical plate screw internal fixation. I keep things minimally invasive and, with less damage to the bone and surrounding musculature, that helps both surgical times and shortens recovery."

"So, tell me what you look for when determining which patients are a good fit. What makes Mrs. Upton a good fit, in particular?"

Stella launched into a very technical explanation of patient criteria and a discussion of how the traditional surgical implants were less effective than her procedure. Aiden seemed to be following along, so she continued on through her explanation. Surely, he'd stop her if he wasn't able to keep up.

A short while later, the hospital took Mrs. Upton upstairs to her room. Aiden pulled Stella to the side, his hand lingering on her arm a bit too long to be purely professional. The simple touch sent a wave of interest burning up her arm and into her core.

"Usually my involvement ends when they head upstairs, but I'd like to follow her case and see how it goes moving forward. I'd like to observe when you perform her surgery, if that's okay?"

"Of course. I'll be getting that scheduled as soon as she's cleared for anesthesia with that concussion. I'll let you know."

His lips turned up at the corners. "You did good work today with Mrs. Upton."

"You don't have to sound so surprised, Dr. Cook." His compliment paired with that hint of a smile emboldened her, and she nudged him playfully. "Did you think I got sent here only because of my experience in television?"

Aiden's silence was answer enough. The lack of denial spoke to his beliefs as much as direct words ever could. His skepticism created a gulf between them that had her stepping back as if he'd slapped her.

"You did." Stella stared at him, completely stunned. Taking a step back, she put some physical distance between them. She'd grown to expect that sort of thing from other doctors, but somehow, she'd thought Aiden was different. Or maybe the attraction burning between them had simply made her more sensitive to any cynicism coming from him. "I suppose that explains the cold shoulder at the airport. You were resentful of being saddled with me as you presumed me to be incompetent. Wow."

"Stella, I…uh…" Aiden fumbled for words. "I may have had concerns that you would either pass off the hard cases or need to pull out a textbook to look up how to treat them."

His assumptions left her feeling as though she'd been doused with ice water. Determination filled her, warming her back with a fiery need to show him that she was more than a celebrity doctor. "It's fine. But I will prove to you that I'm here because I deserve to be, not just because a television producer thought I'd be ideal for this documentary."

She'd been proving herself her entire life. Everyone made assumptions about her, depending on how much of her past they knew. If they'd seen her on *Britain's Brightest* or *Stay Smart with Stella*, they liked to toss trivia her way, as if having a high IQ meant her brain was full of bits of useless knowledge. If they'd seen the self-filmed show she'd created and starred in throughout college and medical school, they had seen her minimize her intelligence while trying to date the wrong guys. Even now that she had taken on the guest slot at *Good Morning United Kingdom*, they stereotyped her into the role of TV doctor who was more polish than grit.

"Stella, I—"

"I said it was fine, Dr. Cook." She narrowed her eyes at him. Aiden Cook was a complication she didn't have time for. She had too many things on her plate over her remaining seven-and-a-half weeks in Toronto, and she certainly didn't want to waste a single second more than she had to on a man who couldn't be bothered to give her half a chance.

"So, I'm back to Dr. Cook then?" Aiden rose to his full height and crossed his arms over his chest. He stared down at her, his eyes hard and his expression grim. "Listen, Dr. Allen—"

"I see you two are getting along swimmingly." Dr. Stone interrupted whatever tirade Aiden was about to launch into as she walked up.

"We are doing just fine," Aiden countered grumpily.

"And yet I have already heard complaints about you not allowing the film crew to work? And that you and Dr. Allen are squaring off in my corridors, although if rumors are to be believed, you can't decide if you want to kiss her or throttle her."

"I'd quit before I kissed her and I don't want to be on camera." Aiden looked so aghast at the idea of kissing her that Stella nearly flinched.

"Good, then you won't mind spending some time next weekend showing Dr. Allen some of what Toronto has to offer."

"I'm sorry, what?" Aiden seemed as thrown off as Stella did.

"You heard me." Dr. Stone smirked at them. "But I'll repeat myself on the off chance that you didn't. I want you to take Dr. Allen out next Saturday and show her around Toronto.

That gives her some time to settle in. I'm sure by then she'll be ready to get out and about a bit."

"Not sure that's a good idea," Aiden argued.

"We had a deal, did we not?"

Aiden eyed the director before finally nodding. "I'll do my part, Dr. Stone. You don't have to worry about that."

Stella's chin dropped. She wasn't sure exactly what deal Aiden had made with the medical director, but it must have been a doozy for him to agree to settle down so quickly.

"By the way, how's the Christmas party planning coming along?" Dr. Stone raised an eyebrow.

Aiden and Stella both remained quiet.

"I see." Dr. Stone shook her head. "I think it would do you two some good to find some common ground on neutral turf. Plan this party. It's going to be on film, after all. You don't want it to look slapped together at the last minute. Get to know each other."

"Why would you want him to take me out when he clearly has so low an opinion of me?" Stella asked.

"I never said anything of the sort." Aiden

leaned her direction, and his voice dropped lower and took on this sexy, gravelly tone that made her knees weak. “So, what do you say, Stella? Are you up for spending the day with me next Saturday? I could pick you up at nine in the morning.”

Stella’s heart thudded against her chest both at the nearness of the man and the enticement in his words. She was not here for romance; that was a fact. But she certainly wasn’t opposed to spending a day with a handsome man. Even if he was prone to the sulks and mercurial as all get-out.

Words escaped her though. She nodded her agreement.

“Perfect. I’ll see you then.” He sauntered away without a backward glance. His free and easy gait showed no remaining stress on his part from their argument, as if it hadn’t affected him as much as it had her.

She stared after him. How had she gone from being angry with him for believing the worst of her to agreeing to a date of sorts within the space of a moment? So much for her determination to stay as far from Aiden as humanly possible. He'd rendered her speechless when he asked her to spend Saturday with him. They both knew she was only in Toronto for two short months. They were both single, and the chemistry flying between them was nuclear. Although they'd had their hands forced by the medical director, they were both fighting the attraction hard.

What could one day hurt? Hopefully those didn't become famous last words.

"He's not so bad once you get to know him." Dr. Stone gave her a knowing smile.

Stella's estimation of the medical director jumped up a notch when she realized just how deftly the woman had manipulated both Stella and Aiden with only a few well-placed comments. She'd have to watch herself around Dr. Stone or she might well find herself in more unpleasant situations than an obligatory outing with a handsome doctor. Her lips turned up in the barest hint of a smile. She loved a good challenge.

"I can't say that I've seen much to like about him just yet," Stella argued.

Except maybe every inch of him...

"You might find that he's like one of those prickly cacti that has the most beautiful blooms if you can put up with the thorns long enough to see it."

CHAPTER SIX

STELLA HAD NO IDEA what sort of day Aiden had in mind for them when he'd been strong-armed by his boss to spend the day with her. She scrounged through the meager wardrobe she'd brought with her across the ocean. She had scrubs, business suits and loungewear mostly. Why hadn't she brought more casual, going-out sort of clothes!

She pulled on the one pair of jeans that she'd brought, shimmying as she tugged them up over her hips. Jeans and a sweater would have to do, since nothing else she'd brought was appropriate. She shifted side to side as she viewed her full-length look in the mirror. The dark shade of the denim helped make her curves look more desirable and less like Stella was a carb junkie. The deep plum cashmere sweater fell nicely and had the bonus of being exquisitely comfortable. Minimal makeup finished off her look.

Before she could second-guess her choice of outfit, there came a knock on her door. Running a shaky hand over her hair, she smoothed it one last time before answering. She hadn't been this nervous about a date in a decade.

It's not a date, Stella.

When she opened the door though, her heart sank. Confusion filled her thoughts. Aiden had brought Jamie with him?

So it definitely wasn't a date.

Somehow it had never occurred to her that he might bring his son. She'd never spent any time with a single dad before so she wasn't sure of the typical procedures and timelines, but it seemed to her that he'd want to get to know her before involving her in his son's life.

She replayed the conversation in her head, especially after the way they had flirted before that trauma. He hadn't asked her out, no, but they'd been heading that way, hadn't they? His boss had just given them a nudge in the direction they were already moving. Nowhere along the way had he mentioned bringing his son along though.

She gathered herself and smiled at the little

boy. "Hello there, Jamie. I didn't expect to see your sweet face today."

Aiden had the decency to grimace. He ran a hand over the boy's hair in a calm and reassuring manner. "I thought we could see the Toronto Christmas Market and try to get some ideas for the Holiday party. It's family friendly. I didn't think it would be an issue to bring him along."

Grump mode reactivated.

With each word he spoke, tension increased in his frame. Aiden's sensitivity when it came to his son was off the charts. How she handled the next few minutes could determine the course of her next few weeks in Toronto. If she messed this up, Aiden would be against her and her life would be infinitely more difficult and far less fun.

She reached out and touched Aiden's hand to reassure him. "It's fine. It was merely unexpected. Forgive me if I made it seem otherwise. If we're still on, I'll grab my coat and be ready to go."

At his nod, she slipped into her coat and grabbed her wallet and keys from her purse. She placed them in the inner pocket of her coat. She didn't want to cart her purse around all day if they were going to be doing a lot of walking.

"Tell me about this Christmas Market."

"It's an annual event. It opened this week. Usually it runs from November through Christmas, and since we have to plan this party, I thought that maybe the market could provide some inspiration." Aiden put his hand on the small of her back and guided her to the elevator.

Though she couldn't feel the heat from his hand through the layers she wore, the gesture warmed her, nonetheless. Stella enjoyed the feel of Aiden close to her. He was near enough to make her feel protected, but left enough space to avoid crowding her. Aiden invaded her personal space just enough to make her hyperaware of his every movement. The nearness filled her mind with the sorts of ideas she'd been unsuccessfully fighting since she'd met him at the airport.

Don't forget his boss quite literally forced him to ask you out.

The market was only a short drive from Stella's apartment, and Aiden's car was still blissfully warm. Jamie sat quietly in the backseat, just like when they'd picked her up at the airport.

Why was the child so quiet all the time? Every kid she'd ever been around had been unbearably loud and bounced from idea to idea. Jamie's somber countenance confused her. She had so many questions, but dare she ask them? Aiden armored up whenever his son became the topic of conversation and she didn't want to push her luck again with him.

The crowd size at the market gave Stella a bit of a surprise. Somehow, she hadn't expected it to be such an event. She'd pictured a small craft market with lots of handmade goodies to peruse. Even before they were fully within the boundaries of the market, she could see it was so much more than a simple craft show. This could only be considered a full-on event.

Jamie pointed at the life-size gingerbread houses with an expression of awe. Stella wasn't entirely sure she didn't have the same look of amazement on her own face. Life-size gingerbread houses were impressive. Were they actually gingerbread or only painted to look so?

She made a mental note to find out before the day was through.

"If you like the gingerbread houses, we could maybe do something with them for decorations?"

"Hmm... It is a possibility, of course."

"One that you don't like, even though you like those particular gingerbread houses. Got it." The confusion in his voice said that he didn't understand why she'd seemed noncommittal though.

"I don't want the party to appear childish," she offered as explanation. This event was going to be televised. They wanted it to feel upscale and highlight the best of St. Matthew's, without being formal. Gingerbread houses were a touch too informal, however.

The scent of spices wafted through the air. "Mmm... Mulled wine," Stella murmured, wrapping her gloved hand around Aiden's arm. "Can you smell it?"

He tensed under her touch, but didn't pull away. Should she put a more professional level of distance between them?

"I'm more of a craft beer guy myself, but if you want a mulled wine, then we'll find out where they're selling it. If we have the party on hospital grounds, I'm not sure they'll want us to serve alcohol, or else I'd suggest we add that to the party menu."

"Sadly, I believe you are correct on that. We'll have to do something nonalcoholic. They do want us to have something child-friendly though in case anyone brings their family."

Aiden looked down at Jamie. His love for the child shone in his eyes, as bright and clear as the sky that beautiful November morning. "Maybe some hot chocolate? You like hot chocolate, don't you, buddy?"

Jamie nodded somberly. Not even the idea of hot chocolate drew a smile from him.

Stella worried her lower lip as she considered the boy. She couldn't help but notice that he had few of the typical reactions of a child his age.

"Stop that," Aiden warned, his voice low and firm. "I can see where your thoughts are going and that's not going to be a conversation we will be having today."

"You have no idea what I'm thinking," Stella argued. But she was quite sure that he did. He'd caught her inquisitive looks at his son and was cutting her off before she could ask the questions that sat burning on the tip of her tongue.

"Whatever conclusions you've drawn, I guarantee they are wrong." He looked like he might say more, but he buttoned up tight after a quick glance down to his son. In the way he hesitated, she could see it was private. Maybe he didn't want Jamie to hear whatever it was so didn't feel comfortable talking about it with the child present.

"Oh…" Stella pointed, changing the subject. "Look at that."

Aiden looked in the direction she pointed and she hoped he'd see something interesting. Her goal had been to lighten the swiftly darkening mood and to take Aiden's attention off her interest in his son.

"What?" he asked. "The carolers?"

"Hmm… Yes." She answered without delay even as she scanned the christmas market quickly for the carolers he was looking at. "Christmas carols are one of my favorite parts of the holiday. Do you think perhaps we could incorporate caroling into our party?"

At least she didn't have to try to lie. She wasn't very good at being dishonest. In fact, the slightest lie would have her face lighting up like a neon sign. She may have grown up on camera, but she'd never be a Hollywood star, despite having had a few offers over the years.

"I think that's a great idea. If you love carolers, you will love this then. Follow me." Aiden guided Jamie through the crowd, never releasing the boy's hand. Stella stayed close to him, occasionally letting her fingers clutch loosely at his sleeve. "The carolers here are fantastic."

Thankfully, there'd been something interesting off in the vicinity she'd gestured. It would have been beyond embarrassing had there been nothing but a wall. She hadn't even looked before she raised her hand.

Aiden stopped at a booth just before they reached the carolers. He waved a hand at the confections in front of them. "Do you want some?"

Graham crackers, chocolate and marshmallows covered the table. Stella shook her head. She had never had much of a sweet tooth. "I'm good, thanks. I love the idea of having s'mores at the party, but I don't think admin would be permissive of open flames, do you?"

"Nope. Maybe a cookie-decorating station

though? Something to keep people around for a while and keep the kids busy?"

"Hmm, that idea has potential." Cookie decorating was far more practical than gingerbread houses. This was something they could really work with, actually. It wouldn't be expensive either.

"You sure you don't want any?" He gestured again at the s'mores ingredients in front of them.

"I really couldn't."

"Your loss. What about you, little man?" he asked Jamie. "You want some, don't you?"

Jamie nodded, the smallest of smiles turning up his lips.

Aiden purchased supplies to make s'mores and a couple skewers. Where did he plan on making them though?

That question quickly found its answer.

A row of firepits ran the length of the performance area. A few were occupied with families roasting marshmallows and warming their hands against the crisp cold of the day.

Aiden claimed one of the empty firepits and began showing Jamie how to roast marshmallows. Somehow, the man gave his son the space and freedom to learn a new skill while simultaneously ensuring that the child was safe. His interactions with his son showed a softer side to the brooding doctor who she found endlessly attractive.

In that moment, the thought flittered briefly through her mind that family life might not be so bad. There was a certain allure to spending the day almost as a family, although she hesitated to slot herself into the maternal role. With no cameras and no publicity, there was none of the falsehood she'd grown up with.

Her parents loved her—of that she had no doubt. They'd also loved the spotlight. Her mother in particular had thrived under the attention that Stella's television career had brought her. Stella always thought it was like having two mothers, really. The overbearing one bossed Stella around behind closed doors, but the cameras brought out the lovely mum who seemed so perfect and ideal.

The carolers started a new song, enthralling Stella with their harmonizing. Closing her eyes, she relaxed. As she let the music pull her in, the thoughts of her mother drifted out. The harmony washed over her and tension slipped from her as she swayed along with the beat. The music dropped off and Stella opened her eyes reluctantly.

"Thank you for listening to the Candy Cane Carolers! We're going to take a quick break to warm up and we'll be back soon. Enjoy your day at Toronto Christmas Market," the lead caroler announced.

Stella sighed. They'd been so lovely that she hated to see their performance end. Maybe there would be time to catch another carol or two before they went home for the day though.

She looked to see if Aiden and Jamie had enjoyed the caroling, but they'd put their entire focus into building s'mores. Crouched down next to Jamie, Aiden helped the little boy with his snack. He even produced a wet wipe from one of his pockets to clean the excess marshmallow from Jamie's face and hands. What else did he have stashed in those pockets?

A shiver ran through her and she stepped closer to the firepit. She held her hands over the flames, trying to warm her chilled extremities. "It's so chilly today," she said to Aiden.

He chuckled. "Today's rather warm for November, actually. I take it the weather's not so cold where you're from."

"This is warm?"

"This is warm," he confirmed with a grin that sent her stomach aflutter.

What have I gotten myself into?

Not just the trip to Toronto and all the associated stress, but this connection with Aiden had the potential to be life altering. Her analytical brain was working overtime to analyze all the possible outcomes that these circumstances opened up.

"You two ready to do some shopping?" Aiden picked Jamie up and held out a hand to Stella. "The crowd is rather thick over here. Wouldn't want to get separated, after all."

Stella slid her hand into his. Despite the chill in the air, with Aiden's hand clasped around hers, she no longer shivered from the cold. Warmth spread from her hand and throughout her body. Why did she have to react so strongly to him?

They spent the next couple hours walking slowly from booth to booth. They discussed ideas along the way as inspiration jumped out at them. They'd settled on doing something simple, but traditional. Aiden was vehemently against bringing anything that glittered into the hospital, arguing that they had to give the janitorial staff a break. Stella had to concede when he brought up that point. Glitter was beautiful, but it did make a mess and she didn't want to pile work on any department at Christmas.

When they came upon a small play area, Jamie's eyes lit up. He pointed with as much excitement as she'd ever seen from him.

"You want to play for a little while?"

Jamie nodded shyly.

"Do you mind?" Aiden asked.

"Me?" Stella shook her head. "Of course not! Let him have some fun."

In fact, she rather hoped to see the little boy play. She'd love to see a true smile on his solemn little face. Each of the shy looks he'd given her had already helped him worm his way into her affections.

"Go ahead," Aiden told his son.

Standing by the only opening to the play area, Stella shivered as the little boy ran to a castle anchored in the middle of the playground.

"Dr. Allen, I do believe we will need to get

you a warmer winter coat." Aiden took his scarf off and draped it around Stella's neck. His body heat still clung to the knitted garment. "At least until you grow a thicker skin and get used to the weather here in Toronto."

"It's been two weeks here and I've yet to adjust." Snow flurries floated softly in the air and she could see her breath with each exhale. She raised an eyebrow at him. "How exactly does one get used to freezing their toes off?"

He brushed a stray bit of hair back from her face. Lifting one shoulder in a casual shrug, he replied, "I was raised here. I hardly notice it. How are you liking Toronto so far?"

"Busy." Stella turned her attention back to his son who was waving at them from behind the Plexiglas barrier on the second level of the play structure. "Jamie seems to be having an amazing time."

"Is he the only one?" Aiden asked.

"No, today has been quite lovely." Stella glanced over at him, surprised to see that he was watching her. She gave him a wry smile. "The only way today could be better were if it were warmer. I'm freezing even with your kind loan of your scarf."

Aiden stepped closer. His body heat enveloped her and the next shiver that coursed down her spine had nothing to do with the cold air around them. She licked her suddenly dry lips and Aiden's eyes dropped to her mouth.

Kissing Stella was a perfectly acceptable response to the way her tongue teased out over her lower lip, surely. He slid one arm around her waist and pulled her close. Her soulful green eyes had caught his attention in the airport, and even when they glittered dangerously with anger, he'd been intrigued and aching to kiss her.

"Help!" someone screamed.

Aiden pulled away from Stella and moved in the direction of the pleas for assistance. A woman was standing next to a little boy who was lying fairly still on the rubberized flooring of the play area.

"What happened?" he asked, switching into emergency physician mode.

"He fell from the top," she squalled, her words almost unintelligible in her panic.

Aiden glanced up to see that was about six

feet. The little one was maybe four. Far too big a height for him to be comfortable.

"Stella, can you take care of Jamie?" he asked over his shoulder, knowing instinctively that she'd be standing there.

"I've got him. You take care of this wee one."

Gently, his fingers kneaded and prodded the child's bones and muscles. No obvious breaks or deformities. That was good. He breathed a sigh of relief when the child began to move on his own and cried out for his mommy.

"Hey, buddy, look here at me." Aiden used the flashlight app on his phone to check the boy's pupils. They were uneven and the left was slow to react.

Crap.

"Has someone called the paramedics?" he asked calmly. He'd learned years ago never to let it show that he had concerns about a patient. That was the quickest way to having a panicked family member go nuts.

When he got an affirmative reply, he returned to examining his young patient. Pediatrics wasn't his specialty, but this kid clearly had a head injury.

"Does your head hurt?"

The kid nodded and then grabbed for his head. "Ow!"

"I know it hurts. Is anything numb or tingly?" No response. "Can you see me okay? Am I blurry or fuzzy?" Again, no reply.

The paramedics came rushing up then, and Aiden turned his little patient over to their capable hands. He took a few minutes to give them the information he had, and his concerns, but let them do their jobs and didn't try to tell them what to do. He hated when people came into his ED and tried to tell him how to do his job, so he wouldn't do it to the paramedics.

They quickly ushered the little boy into the ambulance and sped away with the lights and sirens going. They needed to get the child there quickly so that a neurosurgeon could get a look at him.

Once they were out of sight, Aiden turned to look for Stella and Jamie. He couldn't help the smile when his eyes landed on them. They were sitting together on a nearby bench and Jamie was snuggled into Stella's arms. He had popped his thumb into his mouth. His eyes were closed and it looked like he might nap right there in her arms.

"Hey," he said as he walked up to them. "Thanks for looking out for him."

"Oh, it was no problem at all." Stella sighed. Her face relaxed into a look of utter contentment. "I think he likes me."

Aiden sucked in a breath. His little boy craved the attention of a woman in his life. He hadn't realized how much until he saw how readily Jamie took to Stella and sought her approval. Thoughts of getting Stella back in his arms and kissing her were whisked away on a wave of guilt.

He hadn't expected Jamie to bond with her so quickly. Or even at all… Jamie had been slow to warm up to everyone Aiden had introduced him to. He'd been slow to warm to Aiden, even.

Not that Aiden hadn't been understanding of Jamie's reticence.

After the way Britney had just abandoned him, it was a surprise that the little boy could trust enough to bond with anyone. Aiden swallowed hard at the memory of the first time he'd met his son, pushing the darkness back.

If he allowed himself to go down that line of treacherous thoughts, it would ruin an otherwise good day.

"He's tired. We should go so I can get him home for a nap." It was best to get Jamie home and away from Stella before he got any further attached.

Stella gave him a look that said she was aware of his intentions, but she agreed.

They walked slowly to the parking lot. The way Jamie clung to Stella when they went to leave the market made Aiden worry. Jamie hadn't wanted to get in his car seat at all, asking Stella to keep holding him. In an attempt to pacify the child, Stella had climbed into the rear seat with him.

Rather than reassure Aiden, her actions only kicked his concern into high gear. Had he made a real mistake bringing Jamie along today? Stella was only going to be in Toronto temporarily, after all. Stabs of regret spiked through his heart. He should have considered that Jamie might form an attachment.

He stood outside the car and gathered his thoughts. Was it fair to his son for Aiden to be introducing him to women? Aiden certainly had no intentions of beginning anything that might become permanent. Long-term wasn't a relationship status he'd ever wanted applied to himself, but particularly not now that he was a father.

After climbing into the car, he started the engine and backed out of the space. The drive to Stella's apartment was made in silence on his part. Stella and Jamie talked softly in the seat behind him while he brooded on the mistakes he'd made that day.

He hadn't even considered that bringing Jamie along would be potentially problematic. Initially, his thought had been that the christmas market would be a good low-pressure situation where they could spend the day and get some ideas for the employee party. And that Jamie might be a good buffer since their conversations were often volatile. The idea that Jamie might get attached so quickly hadn't even occurred to him. Aiden wanted to kick himself for not thinking of the possibility. It was why he hadn't dated since Jamie had come into his life, after all.

When he pulled into the parking garage at

Stella's temporary abode, he stepped out of the car to talk to her briefly. He needed to make her understand how today was not going to happen again. "Today was a mistake," he said bluntly.

Hurt flashed over her features before she shut down all emotion. "Was it?"

Hurting her hadn't been his goal, and he wanted to take her in his arms and soothe the pain he'd just caused with his bald statements. He even took a step closer to her, but he couldn't embrace her like he wanted. How could he both hold her close and push her away?

"You're leaving." He shrugged, as if that were explanation enough.

"And?" Stella raised a brow in question. "This isn't brand-new information that you've only just learned. In fact, you knew the details of my stay in Toronto before I did. I'm uncertain as to why it's suddenly a problem though. You nearly kissed me. You had no problem with that, at least until Jamie fell asleep in my lap. Are you pulling away because you realized that I might be developing a bond with your son?"

He swallowed hard. How could he explain what he was so conflicted about? He wanted her, but he wanted her at arm's length. The only valid defense he could verbalize was to protect his son. "Jamie can't get attached to someone who is leaving."

And neither can I.

The words hung between them, becoming a suddenly impenetrable force separating them. It percolated while they stared at each other, neither blinking, neither seeming to want to look away.

After a moment, Stella caved. "I see," she said softly. "I'll take my unwanted presence to my apartment. Thank you for today. It was wonderful despite the harsh ending."

The stiffness in her back as she walked away from him highlighted how much pain he'd caused her. He sucked in a fast breath. For a moment, he wished that she had known him when he had been fun loving and didn't carry such burdens. But he could wish all night and not change a thing. He wasn't that man anymore. And it wasn't all about him anymore. The walls around his heart had to be strong enough to protect more than himself now. He also had to protect Jamie.

He couldn't let in another woman who was destined to leave.

CHAPTER SEVEN

"DOES POOR MRS. UPTON know that her surgeon isn't really a surgeon, she just plays one on TV?" one of the nurses tittered as Stella came into the operating room.

She released a shaky breath and tried not to react. Bone-weary exhaustion had settled over her an hour ago and she hadn't been able to break free of it. After her unexpected non-date date with Aiden, she'd struggled with insomnia all weekend and had started the week off with a sleep deficit. Between the lack of real rest and the stress of presenting a series of lectures all about the surgical technique she'd developed, she was nearly done in.

She hadn't realized just how much harder it would be to share her technique with surgeons in a different country. There wasn't even a language barrier to contend with, yet each presentation somehow siphoned energy off her like a parasite. Four lectures so far this week had really drained her.

Stella needed this surgery. The boost of energy she always got from performing a complicated surgery would go a long way.

"I'm surprised there's not a camera crew in here." Another nurse snorted.

She paused in front of them and raised an eyebrow.

One of them had the decency to look ashamed of himself, but the other gave her a smirk. "Where are the hair and makeup crews, Dr. Hollywood?"

"Gave them the day off, I'm afraid." She forced a smile. As usual, her defenses were going up because people thought she was all fluff and no substance. In her head, she gave herself a bit of a pep talk.

You can do this, Stella. It's no different than any other day in your life. Show them that you are here on merit and not just because a producer liked your face.

"That's enough," a third nurse said. Her name was Gemma and Stella was growing quite fond of her. They'd worked a couple surgeries together and Stella thought they might become friends. "She's fully qualified and now that she's been here for three weeks, all of you know it. And if it wasn't the television program you were fussing about, it would be something else."

She sent Gemma a soft smile, thanking her for her confidence. At least one person in the room thought she could do her job. If she could bank the number of times she'd heard the bit about only playing a surgeon on television, she'd be richer than the queen.

"Dr. Allen, I'm looking forward to seeing exactly why you are here."

"Thank you, Gemma. Now, if you ladies and gentlemen are done gossiping, let's get to work, shall we?" Stella gave the chattering nurse a hard look. "Mrs. Upton's poor pelvis won't fix itself and I'm the only one in the room qualified to do it. Unless you've gotten a medical degree in the past few minutes? No?"

The other woman paled behind her mask.

Take that, gossipy cow.

The prejudice against her over her television background had long ago grown old. Still, she was determined not to let them see that they had gotten a rise out of her. When they saw that she was affected by them, it let them win. And Stella was far too competitive to let them win.

She checked with the anesthesiologist and received his nod that they were good to go. With a deep centering breath, Stella made the first incision.

"Now, for those of you watching from the gallery, you might be aware that there are two typical options for a surgical repair in this kind of break—external fixation and internal fixation. What I'm going to show you today is a form of internal fixation, although not the traditional way you might have learned during your surgical rotation. Mrs. Upton's had a small procedure a few days after her fall to stabilize, but now I'll be going in to do the permanent fix."

As she continued through the surgery, she described the techniques in detail for the growing crowd watching from above. While she might have felt a little unease at the start, thanks to the rumors one particular nurse was trying to spread, it didn't take her long to get into the zone. There was nowhere on earth Stella had more confidence than in an operating room.

If she could lecture from the OR each time, rather than from behind a lectern, it would be so much easier.

Deftly, she handled each incision and the placement of each bit of hardware. Her moves were careful, practiced. She prided herself on the precision of her surgical capabilities. When she was operating, nothing rattled her. With a scalpel in her hand, Stella didn't care at all what rumors might be spread. She was unbothered by what others thought.

If only she could carry that confidence over outside the operating room.

"Like the other forms of pelvic fixation, the goal with this is realignment and stability of the displaced fracture. Getting the fracture well aligned is the first step in a successful surgery and leads to the best possible outcomes."

"Are the surgeries always performed under general anesthesia?" one of the doctors in the gallery asked over the intercom.

"Indeed, they are," Stella confirmed.

"In cases of severe trauma, does having to wait to perform this surgery affect the outcome?"

"Overall stability is of course the first goal.

With this particular patient, we needed to wait a bit as she also had quite the concussion from her fall and there was some risk to putting her under anesthesia. Ideally, the surgery is performed as soon as possible after the break."

Aiden slipped into the gallery a few minutes after Stella's surgery was scheduled to begin. The ED had been busy and he'd been unable to get away. He wasn't sure he'd be able to stay for her entire operation, but he'd taken his lunch break with the intent of spending it seeing as much of her work as he could.

He owed her that at least, after the harsh way he'd spoken to her over the weekend, but he hadn't been able to find a way to make the overture. Showing interest in her work seemed like a start, and he hoped to find a way to build on that. Sinking quietly into a seat in the back row, he waited for Stella to resume speaking.

Aiden listened to the joking and the rumbles about Stella being all polished presentation. When one took the joking a bit too far, Aiden felt the need to call him out.

"Hush. Let her work before you try to slam her skills."

The chastised surgeon looked like he wanted to argue, but miraculously kept his mouth shut for the moment.

The gallery quickly quieted as she began to work. Soon, the whispers began again, but this time because they were in awe of her techniques.

Stella Allen was a force to be reckoned with and her skills stood proof. Her economy of motion impressed him. Every move was controlled and precise. It was a thing of beauty. Down in the OR, Stella was speaking, her voice strong and steady as she lectured on the medical techniques she'd pioneered while performing the procedure. Not a speck of weakness or insecurity showed while she was operating. She was flawless.

After the surgery though, she held a little question-and-answer session and he couldn't help but see that she struggled when criticized in any way. Their jabs shot straight to her self-confidence, somehow. Each slight became a barb that she struggled to shake off.

Interesting...

Someone with such a strong connection to the television world should have a thicker skin.

Stella should have been practically bulletproof when it came to criticism after growing up in the public eye, but her mannerisms and discomfort today said otherwise.

In fact, there was a fragility about Stella that drew him to her. He wanted to help her. Protect her.

With every snipe that came at her, his muscles tightened more. With every snide comment, every whispered jab, he found himself leaning farther forward, barely restrained from going after the jerks. He scrubbed a hand over his face in frustration. He barely knew this woman. Where was this relentless protectiveness coming from?

"Dr. Stella, when you filmed these clips did you have a full camera crew? Perhaps an advisor whispering instructions via an earpiece?"

Aiden couldn't take it anymore.

"That is enough!" His voice was louder than he meant it to be, but it silenced the scoffing crowd. "Dr. *Allen*—" he emphasized her proper name and gave it the respect she deserved "—is here to show us something groundbreaking and you stoop so low as to tease her and make childish remarks about her? This is the impression you want to leave of our hospital? I, for one, would like to learn all I can from her. We can't do that if we make it impossible for her to teach. Now, either shut up or get out." Aiden glared until the man backed down.

"I apologize for the interruption, Dr. Allen. Please, continue."

Stella beamed at him and he knew in that moment that any fallout he would face for standing up for her would be worth it. It was a given fact that she was leaving in only five weeks. That alone should be enough reason for him to keep his distance. But he found himself drawn to her, despite knowing she was only there temporarily.

There were a few more questions, which she answered deftly when no one was looking down on her for her career choices. Aiden made his way downstairs and waited around outside the OR so that he could try to steal a moment alone with Stella.

He propped a shoulder against the wall and waited for her to come his direction.

"Thank you," she said softly as she drew close. "You might have noticed, but I was a bit uncomfortable there."

Aiden snorted. "I think it was a little more than that."

She sighed. "I've just given you my thanks—please don't make me want to take it back."

He reached out and gently took one of her hands in his. "I wasn't trying to rub your nose in it. It actually surprised me to see how much you were struggling. I'd have thought you'd be so used to it that it wouldn't even faze you anymore."

Stella grimaced. "One would think that, yes, but it's really quite the opposite. I think I'm rather more sensitive about being teased over anything connected with television. I'm always worried that I've only gotten my foot in the door due to my past. I want to succeed because of my medical skill, not because my mum shoved me into a television program when I was just a child."

"My mom shoved me into Scouts Canada when I was younger. Said it was important for a boy to learn the skills they taught."

"And have you used those skills as an adult?" Stella asked, looking slightly amused at his uneven comparison of their childhoods.

"Actually, yes. I make a mean s'more. Jamie

loved them, even if you were too uptight to enjoy one." He flashed her a grin. "Seriously, though, I made some good friends and the leadership skills have served me well. Even if I don't go camping on the regular, it's not a bad thing to know how to build a fire or set up a tent."

"I suppose not," Stella said. "My mum wasn't a fan of anything of that sort. Not enough recognition from others, you see."

"Your mom seemed so devoted on screen."

"Of course. She couldn't look bad on camera." Stella gave him a wry smile. "In real life she wasn't always the mother she portrayed on screen."

"I was adopted," Aiden found himself saying. He never offered up that information about himself to anyone.

"But you ended up with a loving family?"

"After a while in foster care, yes." His adoptive family had been the one constant in his life and he was lucky to have found them when he did. The Cooks were attentive, loving, generous and a million other positive descriptors. They'd showered him with love from the moment he walked through their door as a hurting nine-year-old, afraid to let his guard down. Even with all they'd done for him, something had always felt like it was missing. But despite the lingering fear of abandonment he'd been left with by his birth parents, Aiden had been raised by some amazing people. He *knew* he was loved. "Overwhelmingly so at times."

"I fully understand the concept of having an overwhelming mother." The warm tinkle of laughter from Stella made him want to take her in his arms.

He even started to reach for her, but at the last second, Aiden covered the move with a glance at his watch. His lunch break was long over. Honestly, he was surprised he'd made it this long without getting called back to the emergency department. He might be pushing his luck by stretching it out any more, yet he found himself asking for more time with Stella.

"Can I buy you a coffee?"

CHAPTER EIGHT

STELLA'S PHONE RANG before she could say yes to the coffee. She winced at the name on the screen. The producer for the program was calling again. He'd called twice during her lecture, so she really shouldn't put him off again. "I'm sorry, Aiden. Can I take a rain check on the coffee? Afraid I have to take this."

"Sure." Aiden took a step back. He kept the smile on his face, but he couldn't hide the disappointment in his eyes. "You know where to find me."

Frustration filled her as he turned and walked away, but she really had to take the call. Martin was not a patient man, and if he got too put out about the delay in response, he might drop out of the project.

"Hello," she answered, just in time to keep the call from switching over to voice mail.

"Stella, this is Martin O'Connor. I've been trying to reach you for hours. I was worried that perhaps I'd gotten the time difference wrong when I kept getting your voice mail. I received the footage you've sent in so far for the Christmas special and I've had some thoughts."

"Hi, Martin, thank you for getting back to me. I was in surgery all morning and have only just finished." Holding her phone with her shoulder, Stella stepped into a nearby consultation room. People who took private telephone calls in public venues drove Stella mad. "Is something wrong with the material you've received so far?"

"Hmm…" he stalled.

Stella's heart rate kicked up at the pause. Martin was known for delivering negativity with a dramatic flair. Sinking down into a chair, she closed her eyes and waited for the bad news to drop.

"I don't want to say that I dislike it, because some of it is quite good. It needs a bit more punch though. Kicking up the drama would certainly add interest for viewers." Martin's voice held a formal quality she'd come to associate with him. Even with a smile on his face, the older man remained distant. He was a brilliant filmmaker though and having him on board was ultimately a good thing.

"Drama?" Stella asked cautiously. Drama could mean so many things, so she needed to get a bit more clarity. He had a vision for the project, clearly, and she wanted to be sure their ideals aligned. Sometimes his ideas stretched beyond her comfort zone though.

"Yes. We need more of you on screen, as well. And, well, I think the best way to add the interest we need is for you to have a love interest." He spoke of her getting a love interest so matter-of-factly that it could have been like he was ordering her to get lunch.

"A love interest?" she repeated, aware that she was sounding like a parrot as she mimicked his words. None of the various scenarios she'd run through her head had involved herself on screen beyond introductions and voice-overs. And romance? Never even the briefest of thoughts. "Martin, that's not the direction that I want to take this program."

"Darling, it's not about what you want, it's about how to bring in an audience."

She cringed at the implication that her love life might draw more viewers than a proper medical documentary. How had her professional documentary about medical staff who worked over the Christmas holidays devolved into a love story? No, she needed to bring this back on track.

"I'm not interested in turning my life into a soap opera! I'm a surgeon and I don't want to look like I'm only paying lip service to my career in medicine." It wasn't the first time she'd been pushed to have a romance on screen. She'd even cooperated while she was in college, but she'd moved beyond that and her focus now was on medicine. "I'm afraid I need to decline."

"Stella, if the program doesn't have anything of real interest, it won't get the needed ratings. And I don't need to remind you how hard it can be to recover from a flop."

Horror filled her at how hard Martin was pushing this angle. She'd wanted to show the world what working in a hospital was like, not give them a reality TV romance. Would she ever have full control over her life or would someone else always be directing her actions?

No.

She wasn't going to stand for this. Her life,

her choice. Stella gritted her teeth. "I am not looking for romance while I'm here. You have to appreciate that I am here to do a job, not find a soul mate."

"It doesn't have to be real. You know how these things go." The director cleared his throat and continued, "Just find a way to bring a touch of spice into it. Something to really draw in the female viewers. They are our biggest demographic for a program of this nature."

"Why me?" Stella asked, despite already knowing the answer.

"You are the star of the show, love." Martin took on the tone of a kindly grandfather explaining something patiently to a child. "We've watched you grow up. We've seen you go off to college and medical school. It's been some time since you've even had a hint of romance on screen. It will be a major draw for the program."

Stella tried not to wince. Being on screen added an extra layer of difficulty to any relationship, as she'd learned the hard way. Now they were asking her to begin a new relationship on camera.

"I appreciate what you're saying, Martin,

but I'm afraid it's a no from me. It wouldn't be right for me to start a relationship when I'm only here a few more weeks." Aiden's face flashed into her thoughts as she repeated the refrain she'd been telling herself about dating him to Martin.

"If you want this program to move forward, you will follow directions." His voice brooked no argument. Clearly, he didn't buy her excuses any more than she did. "I'm not saying you have to marry the fellow, but we do need something more than you've given us. Are you an actress or not?"

"Martin—"

"Stella, darling, it's not really optional. Now if you can't deliver the goods, I'm going to be sending a different videographer out soon. Maybe around the beginning of the month? You know, try to get some different perspectives. Amp up the drama a touch. Makes for better viewing."

"I really feel that's unnecessary," Stella argued.

"We shall see." The line went silent as Martin ended the call.

Putting her own heart, and the heart of another at risk for a temporary fling? It wasn't fair to either her or the other person. Think about faking a romance to improve ratings?

There had to be another way.

She took a deep breath and tried to consider the other options. How could she add drama? Would another romance be enough to satisfy that desire? She might pitch the idea and see. Even as she ran through all the eligible people at the hospital who'd agreed to be on camera for her, she knew it wouldn't work. It would have to be her or the director would never be satisfied.

There was a slight hitch in that plan though. The only man at St Matthew's that she could convincingly pull off even a hint of romance with had refused to be filmed.

Aiden wasn't sure if Stella was avoiding him intentionally over the previous few days or if she honestly hadn't even noticed he was there. This was the first time he'd caught sight of her since his ill-fated attempt at asking her out for coffee. The look of concentration on her face seemed far too intense for an empty hallway in the early morning hours. She didn't acknowledge his presence in the slightest.

Now, Aiden wasn't the sort of man who needed all the attention, but something about her expression concerned him.

"Stella," he called after her.

"Hmm..." She came to a stop and turned to face him. Worry lined her face. Something was definitely bothering her.

"Is everything okay?" He could see that it most certainly was not, but he wasn't sure Stella would want to confide in him.

He wasn't the guy people confided in. He was the reliable guy who they called for a ride if their car broke down. He was the one who people called when they needed a night out or a distraction—at least he had been until Jamie appeared in his life. But he wasn't the guy who people spilled their guts to. He didn't know anyone's deep dark secrets. He never had to worry that he'd let something slip he shouldn't because no one shared that information with him.

Did that mean no one trusted him enough? That thought wasn't a pleasant one to ponder.

He hadn't done anything untrustworthy, so surely not.

Stella flashed him her fake smile.

Yes, he'd learned to tell the difference, but no he wasn't going to consider what that meant. At least not yet.

"You can talk to me, you know." He gave her what he hoped was a reassuring look. For some reason, he actually wanted Stella to confide in him. He wanted to be the man she came to for advice. The feelings that realization brought up in him would have to be unpacked later. At that moment, he had to focus on what Stella needed, not what she made him feel.

Stella opened her mouth as if to speak and closed it quickly like she'd thought better of what she'd been about to say. Indecisiveness showed on her face. White teeth gnawed on her perfectly pink lower lip.

This woman was going to kill him without even trying.

Was murder by lip biting actually a thing?

He reached out a hand, unable to keep from touching her any longer. "What's bothering you?"

"What's not bothering me at this point?" A

harsh exhale combined with a sort of self-deprecating laugh. "I've had to be on my game one hundred percent here, because my televised past gives people the impression that I'm ignorant, despite the programs quite literally having been born because of my intelligence. I have to prove myself time and again. Unfair, really, because I take it on good faith that each and every surgeon I work with is presumed competent yet I'm not afforded the same courtesy."

She paused, but before Aiden could speak, she began again.

"And the program I'm currently filming? The director wants more drama. Not only drama, he wants romance. And not just any romance. He wants *me* to have a romance. I have to find someone to date on camera or there's a very good chance he's going to pull his support for my program."

"You need to date…" He let the words trail off as jealousy surged up from somewhere deep. The idea of another man romancing Stella didn't sit well. Not at all.

"I'll be on camera with you."

He hadn't meant to blurt out those words, but

he couldn't take them back now. And he found he didn't want to. Taking them back meant that he'd have to watch as some other man wined and dined her. He'd have to see her walking the halls of St. Matthew's with her hand on some doctor's arm, that rapt look of attention on another guy's face as she listened carefully to his words.

The stunned look on Stella's face mirrored his own shock at his actions. "You don't want to be on camera though," she said cautiously.

"That's true." Sliding his fingers down her forearm, Aiden gripped her hand and squeezed. "You know what I want less than being on camera?"

She shook her head. With her eyes full of curiosity, Stella waited for him to answer his own question.

"Seeing you with another man," he growled out.

Pink tinted her cheeks. "I see."

"Do you?" He leaned closer, watching as the color in her face deepened. "I have been trying to keep my distance from you, Dr. Allen, but I'm failing at that goal quite miserably."

"Are you saying I make you miserable?"

Stella bristled in faux outrage. The sparkle in her eyes contradicted the would-be anger in her words.

"Very," he said with a grin. "But I can't stay away."

Only their hands were touching, but the moment held an intimacy that couldn't be denied. The tension that rose up between them was something to be savored. Aiden couldn't remember a time when only holding hands with someone affected him this much.

"It needs to just be for show though. I don't date colleagues, no exceptions. And I have to put my son's needs before my own. But you and I both know there could be something here." He gestured between them. "Too much for me to stand by while you flirt with someone else."

She raised an eyebrow. "So, let me get this clear. You want to date me, but only on camera."

"Yes." It might be unfair, but he wasn't going to pretend he didn't have concerns about getting involved. By faking a relationship on camera, he got to get close to her, but the relationship would remain surface level. No depth that put him or his son at risk.

"I see…"

"You get what you want. Take the win. Just don't fall in love with me. I'm not looking for anything real."

"Why do you assume I would fall in love with you?" She crossed her arms over her chest.

He whispered in her ear, "I don't want you to, Dr. Allen. I'm just warning you that there's no future here."

The barest glimpse of desire flickered in her eyes before it was replaced by what could only be called stubbornness. "What if your heart's the one in danger?"

"My heart is locked up tight in a vault surrounded by razor wire."

"Is that so?" Stella snorted. "Well, I can assure you that your heart and your body are both safe from any unwelcome advances from me."

He chuckled. While he had no interest in emotional entanglements, he wouldn't say a physical relationship was unwelcome.

"I find nothing about this situation amusing." Anger flashed in her eyes.

"You think you can resist me for another four and a half weeks, Stella? Even if we have to spend time together on camera, appearing to grow closer and closer." He moved in until millimeters separated them. "We can fake a relationship, but you can't fake your reactions to me. Those are real."

"As are yours to me." She ran her fingers along his jaw and it took all he had to suppress the shudder at her touch.

He wanted to deny it, but it would be a lie.

"Dr. Cook to trauma one, Dr. Cook to trauma one."

The timing of that page was fortuitous. A few more moments, and he might have been goaded into kissing her.

"Saved by the bell?" she joked.

"More like punished." He gave her hand one last squeeze. "Think about what I'm proposing though. Don't go starting an on-camera romance without me today. I'm serious."

What exactly had he gotten himself into by agreeing to be on camera with Stella? He was toeing a line here, faking a relationship with a woman he was really attracted to. The idea of Stella even fake dating someone else rubbed him up the wrong way though.

He'd made the right choice, so why did he feel a little green around the gills about it?

CHAPTER NINE

AIDEN DIDN'T WANT her to date anyone else? And he wanted to be on camera after vehemently refusing? Stella pinched her arm, hard.

Definitely not dreaming. Hmm…

Well, his sudden change of direction was unexpected. And even more so a relief. Drama sold in the television world. Romance was also an audience pleaser. Both would be best. Aiden was the only man she'd met in Toronto who held any interest for her though, so she'd never have been able to convincingly pull off a romance with anyone else. Not even a fake one.

Even though she'd grown up on camera, Stella was no actress. Past directors had gotten so frustrated when she failed to participate as they wished in false narratives. She'd never really mastered the art of subterfuge and she couldn't tell a lie without lighting up like a neon sign.

Honesty was a virtue, right?

Stella rubbed the bridge of her nose, trying her best to wish away the stress headache building behind her eyes. This trip was not turning out how she'd thought it would. It was far more stressful than she'd imagined. The excitement, too, was more than she could have pictured.

All morning, she'd been frazzled, worrying about how she could pull off a fake relationship with any man other than Aiden. Her stomach had roiled and twisted into a giant knot. She drew in a shaky breath. Anxiety had frayed her poor nerves to the point of breaking, and now that worry had all been for naught.

A small giggle bubbled up inside her. She had nearly worried herself ill over a nonissue. Wasn't that just like her?

The arrogance in his eyes when he'd told her not to fall in love with him though made her defenses rise. Who did he think he was? Just because he was absolutely gorgeous did not mean he was irresistible. The way he'd warned her off tempted her to blur the lines between fake and real, to tease him and possibly take him down a peg or two by making him fall for her. Of course, she'd be putting her own heart squarely at risk in order to take him down.

A series of beeps sounded from the phone in her pocket, startling her out of her thoughts. Pulling it out, she read the words on the screen and sighed.

It was a blunt reminder from Martin as to what he expected from her.

Stella, I need the additional footage from you ASAP. Remember to keep it heavy on the drama and the romance. I'm not fussed if it's real or fake, just be sure it's attention-catching.

A second message followed before she could formulate a reply to the first.

And I do mean ASAP if you don't want me to put the brakes on this little pet project of yours.

Stella huffed. There wasn't a chance that she was going to let him kill this program without fighting for it. Now driven with purpose, Stella put her mind toward finding some of the drama and romance that the director wanted to see. It didn't take her long to find a few in-hospital romances where the couples were willing to be filmed and interviewed.

With no presentations to give or surgeries to perform that day, Stella immersed herself in filming. She did short interviews with the participating couples, happily noting that at least some of their answers were dramatic enough to pacify Martin's penchant for excitement.

One of the couples was more than happy to try their skills at acting. Tyler and Gemma excitedly staged a fight in the hallway about how working opposite shifts was putting a wrench in their relationship. Had Stella not been aware that the young couple was acting, she'd have thought a breakup was imminent. Gemma, in particular, was quite convincing and even managed to shed some very real tears.

When Henry turned the camera off, Tyler pulled Gemma in for a kiss. Stella turned away from the heartfelt display in order to give them a bit of well-earned privacy. They'd given her quite a bit of material to work with. It should appease Martin for now.

She moved toward Henry, ready to call it a day with filming. "Shall we take a look at what we managed to collect today?"

He nodded and they reviewed the footage together. While some of it might need some edits, they'd captured a good bit that was usable and Stella was quite pleased with it.

"Leave that out," Aiden called from behind her.

She startled, knocking the camera from Henry's hand when she spun in Aiden's direction. Her fingers managed to gain a grip on the expensive piece of equipment only just in time. "Aiden, you gave me a fright."

"Sorry about that. Let me just have this for a second." He took the camera from her. Nodding at Tyler, he asked, "You mind?"

Henry took the camera from Aiden's outstretched hand. "What do you want me to film?"

"Just keep it pointed at Dr. Allen." Aiden stepped back as Henry lifted the camera and aimed it in Stella's direction as instructed.

Hoping that her smile looked more genuine than confused, Stella waited to see what Aiden was up to. She didn't have to wait long.

"Dr. Allen, might I have a word?" Aiden asked as he stepped up and into the path of the lens.

"Of course, Dr. Cook," she replied, still no less confused. Her heart rate picked up at his nearness.

"Do you have plans for Saturday evening?"

Stella gaped at him. Her mind refused to process the fact that Aiden had not only asked her on a date, but had done so on camera. His gruff refusal to be filmed still held dominance in her mind over his blurted decision this morning. The surprise rendered her speechless.

Gently touching her hand, Aiden prompted for an answer by rephrasing his query. "What do you say to dinner on Saturday?"

Swallowing hard, Stella licked her suddenly dry lips before answering. "I'd love to have dinner with you, Dr. Cook."

Aiden lifted her hand with an exquisite slowness. His breath was hot and his lips tempting as they lightly grazed the tender skin of her wrist. "Then I'll pick you up at seven."

With her heart racing in her chest, Stella stared after him as he walked away. Her hand still burned with the fire he'd started with his breath and lips and she let her hand flutter toward her chest. Resisting that man might be harder than she thought.

"Wow." Henry lowered the camera. "That was…wow. Martin has been waiting all month for a scene like that."

"Indeed," she murmured.

Twinges of guilt still stabbed at him over how he'd brought Stella into Jamie's life without so much as a thought. And how he selfishly wanted to spend an evening alone with Stella. Thankfully, his mom had been enthusiastic about the opportunity to spend the evening with her grandson while he went on a date.

Nerves fluttered around in his stomach, frustrating him to no end. He was a grown man. He shouldn't be as nervous as a teenager about to go on his first date.

It was his first *real* date since finding out he was a father though. The christmas market hardly counted as a date, even before he'd gotten weird and ruined things. Jamie's presence had served as a chaperone and they'd barely even touched. And a few brief coffee breaks together at work in front of an entire hospital certainly weren't dates.

Starting a romance with someone on camera and in full view of his coworkers went against nearly every fiber of his being, but from the moment she'd mentioned that her director wanted her to get involved with somebody he'd had no choice. He couldn't stomach the idea of her being with someone else, of her touching someone else. Not even if it was faked for the camera.

"So, you have a hot date tonight?" his mother asked with a knowing smirk.

"Moms of grown-up sons should never say the words *hot date*." He shuddered at the connotation that left in his mind. Was she trying to put a damper on his evening? Ugh.

"Tell me about her." His mom's eyes twinkled with mischief.

He grumbled in exasperation. "I will tell you about her when there's something to tell. It's a first date. I'm hardly proposing to her."

"Let an old woman have hope." She sniffed, before hugging Jamie tight. "I'm hoping for more grandchildren in the future. Preferably soon when I'm still young enough to enjoy them."

"Can we not have this discussion again tonight?" Aiden sighed. His mom had been angling for grandchildren since shortly after

Aiden had graduated college. He'd been able to push the topic off through medical school and residency, but for the last several years, it had been frequently and passionately brought up. Jamie's appearance had delighted her and now she was eager for Aiden to give Jamie a sibling.

"Only if you tell me about your date," she said, attempting to bargain her way into more information by wearing him down.

"You mean the date that I'm going to be late for if I don't leave soon." The protest was weak, but it was all he had.

She countered his argument swiftly and surely. "All the more reason to tell me quickly."

"You are so stubborn." He could tell by the set of her jaw that she wasn't going to let him leave until he gave her something though. If he held his ground, he'd be late. So he gave in to her demands, giving her a small amount of information. "Her name is Stella. She's an orthopedic surgeon."

"The one you were looking up?"

"Yes. Can we leave it at that for now?"

His mom pursed her lips unhappily, but she nodded. "For now. Will you be home tonight or should I plan to drop Jamie off at day care in the morning?"

"I'll be home tonight," he said. "Can you save the rest of the inquisition for a later date? You wouldn't want her to think I stood her up now, would you?"

"You really like her," his mom said with a look of surprise.

Honestly, he was as surprised as she was that he liked Stella as much as he did. He'd never, ever thought of long-term before her. There was something special about her though that made him crazy, but it could never be anything real since she was leaving soon.

"What are you waiting for then? Get out of here!" His mom practically shoved him out the door. "I won't wait up."

The heat of the chemistry that burned between him and Stella meant he wanted to go home with her, but it was too soon. As he walked to his car, he wondered at that. Too soon for whom? He'd never had a problem taking a woman to bed on the first date before. In fact, that had been the bulk of his past relationships.

Something about Stella though made him

want to take things slower, to savor each interaction. Gut reaction said slow would be worth the wait with her, and Aiden had learned to trust his gut. But fake dates didn't wind up in bed. Fake dates put on a show for the people around them and kept their distance in private. He needed to remember that.

He knocked on Stella's door precisely at seven o'clock. Despite her determination, his mother hadn't succeeded in making him late for his date after all.

The door swung inward and he was at a loss for words. His tongue suddenly too big for his mouth, he tried unsuccessfully to swallow and remember how to talk. She was so beautiful it took his breath away. She'd clearly forgotten that they had plans tonight though, because she stood in front of him wearing flannel pajama bottoms and a tank top.

"Hello," she said, dipping her head shyly and breaking eye contact. The softest pink blush crept up her cheeks.

His confidence spiked when he realized she was as unsure as he was about how to proceed. "I was so much more anxious about tonight than I was about Saturday and the christmas market. Silly, huh, when I show up to find you in pajamas?"

"Oh, thank goodness. I was worried it was just me!" Stella's smile shone brightly enough to light up the Toronto skyline and it took his breath away. "I didn't expect you to actually show!"

The more he flirted with this woman, and the more time he spent with her, the deeper risk he was taking in falling in love with her. He really needed to rein in his emotions, find a way to keep Stella at arm's length, but he couldn't seem to make himself take the necessary steps. He tried to repeat to himself the refrain that this date was a fake, but he was struggling to believe himself.

"I thought we'd go out," he said softly. Rather than stepping back though, Aiden found himself stepping closer. He offered her a smile as he stepped inside the apartment and closed the door behind him. "Unless you'd rather stay in?"

"I didn't think it was a real date," she said as she grabbed a cardigan and covered up her bare shoulders. "Really thought that was all for the camera."

"Don't you think it's best we get to know each other a little? It will help our fake relationship seem a bit more realistic." He shrugged. "How can we bond if we don't spend time together?"

"Bond…"

"Plus, a few of the nurses in the ED are going ice skating tonight. To keep the reactions real, it might be a good idea to be seen out and about together. It would lend some visual weight to the hospital gossip."

"I see." She tilted her head and stared at him for a moment. "Give me a moment to change."

Aiden went to the window and looked down at the street while he waited for Stella to get changed. He almost regretted telling her that they were going to go ice skating where they might bump into some of their coworkers. Those pajamas were going to be missed. The thought of them coming off her in the other room sent him into a vivid daydream. He might avoid emotional attachments like the plague, but he was very pro physical entanglements. Especially with Stella.

"Aiden?" Stella's fingers snapped in front of Aiden's eyes. She stood next to him, her face pensive as she contemplated him. “Where did you go? Clearly, you checked out on me.”

“Hmm… Maybe one day I’ll tell you.”

CHAPTER TEN

THE HEAT IN Aiden's eyes when she caught his attention told her where his thoughts had gone, even if he wouldn't put a name to it. Warmth bubbled up inside her and made her nearly giddy.

While romance hadn't even been a blip on her radar when thinking of this trip to Toronto, she wasn't going to pass up the chance at whatever this was between them. Some things just couldn't be faked, and the chemistry between them was one such thing. Vacation flings were an actual thing, right? Outside her norm, maybe, but normal. Healthy, even, as long as everyone was clear on the boundaries.

But how to bring up the topic of boundaries?

Back home, Stella was known to be rather straightforward and blunt. She liked to know where she stood with people and she preferred to be honest about where people stood with her. Her lack of filter had, on occasion, created problems in her personal life. Still, she liked to be aware of the relationship limits. Crossing an ocean had thrown her off-kilter though, and one spark from Aiden's hand had nearly capsized her.

Stella liked plans. She made daily schedules and her calendar was filled as far in advance as she could do so. Her desk was usually covered in color-coded to-do lists and she liked knowing what to expect personally and professionally. The hours she spent setting goals and visualizing strategies helped make her more confident in her everyday life. She feared her world careening out of control and took every step to minimize the chances of that happening.

Her medical career was the one aspect of her life that had never let her down. She'd worked really hard to have a career that was all hers and not under her mother's influence. Psychologically speaking, her control issues stemmed from her childhood and her relationship with her mother. Being thrust into the spotlight at such a young age, without being asked, had made her value the concept of choice. It had ingrained in her a deep respect of autonomy and she did all she could to avoid infringing on anyone else's freedom of choice. She didn't really know what being a good mum looked like, but her own mother hadn't been the best example. No, it was safest all around if she just focused all her attention on what she could control: her career.

So, what was it about Aiden that made her so willing to relinquish a bit of that hard-earned control? Fake relationship or not, the man intrigued her.

"I know ice skating was chosen because of others going there, but where would you normally take a date?" she prodded, curious to hear how the handsome doctor at her side would usually treat the woman he was taking out for the evening.

Aiden's face tightened. He tugged at his collar. Opening and closing his mouth repeatedly, Aiden ultimately remained silent. The question clearly made him uncomfortable.

He looked so awkward that she took pity on him. "Okay, you don't have to tell me where you take your dates."

"I don't date a lot. The women I do date don't

expect much beyond a nice dinner or drinks and then some…uh…adult activity."

"I see," Stella said, trying her best not to let her mind drift toward engaging in some adult activity with Aiden. "Let's talk about ice skating then. Are there actual outdoor rinks here or is that another televised myth?"

Secretly, Stella loved watching all the sweet romance movies that highlighted the fun of the holiday season. Sometimes, she needed the assurance that a movie would end as expected, not wanting the anxiety of an unknown ending. Given the many romance movies she'd watched, it never failed to amaze her that there was always a place to go skating under the wintry sky. She was really hoping that it would be an outdoor rink.

"Can you skate?" Disbelief colored his voice.

She affected what she hoped was a nonchalant shrug before she replied. "I've been a few times, but I'm not going to be representing my country in the next Olympics."

"I played hockey up through college." Sparks of mischief shone brightly in his eyes. "Think you can keep up?"

"Is that a challenge, Dr. Cook?" She narrowed her eyes in playful competition. While she wasn't very athletic overall, Stella did like to indulge in games and competitive activities. Deep down, she knew she couldn't truly compete with a former hockey player, but she would have fun trying. "Think you can beat me then?"

Aiden's deep, booming laugh sent shivers speed walking down her spine. "I see no way I can lose. I'm confident on the ice. If you can't skate, you'll end up in my arms. If you can, then we can have a true competition. I don't give up easily though."

He opened the car door for her, moving closer to assist her into the vehicle. When he leaned in, her quick exhale filled the space between them. Aiden must have read the burst of desire that rose up at his nearness. His eyes darkened and his own breathing picked up in pace.

"Get in the car, Stella," he said with a groan. "I'm trying to take this slow, but if you keep looking at me like that, we won't be going ice skating. We'll be going back up to your apartment and we might not make it out again until morning."

Her cheeks burned as she swung her legs

fully inside the vehicle. While he walked around to get into the driver's seat, she fanned her blazing hot face. It took all she had not to just invite him back up to her apartment to see if his actions could back his words.

Aiden white-knuckled the steering wheel. "At least being on the ice ought to cool us down."

Stella chuckled at his little joke. "Is that the Toronto version of a cold shower?"

"It'll do the job." He shifted in his seat.

"How long has it been since you've skated?" She hoped that some innocuous conversation might release some of the tension between them. This fake date was feeling far too real at the moment and she wanted to move it back onto more neutral territory.

"It's been a few years," he admitted.

That knowledge gave her a touch of hope that she might not embarrass herself too badly against the former hockey player.

Don't forget that your graceful self landed smack on your bottom twice.

"Hasn't been quite that long for me." She had gone skating only a few months back, so her experience was more recent. She had that to her advantage.

"Don't gloat yet. I used to live at the rink before I traded my blades for a stethoscope."

"Will you teach Jamie to play hockey when he's a bit older?" The image of little Jamie decked out in full hockey gear made her smile. She'd only seen them on television, but children in sports uniforms always looked adorable. "I bet he'd love having an activity to share with his dad."

Aiden grunted. "I hope so. I hadn't thought of starting him in hockey yet. He's been so slow to warm up to anyone and has showed so little interest in anything, really, that it hasn't been a high priority. I've been trying to gain his trust and get him speaking."

"Gain his trust?" That particular turn of phrase caught Stella's attention. While she wasn't a parent, it seemed to her that children instinctively trusted their parents until given a reason not to. She'd certainly trusted her parents as a child. "Why wouldn't your son trust you?"

Aiden pulled the car over and put it into Park. He sat in silence, staring at his hands where they still gripped the steering wheel for so long that she thought he might not answer.

"It took time for me to gain Jamie's trust because he didn't meet me until his second birthday. That's when his mom dropped him off at the hospital with a note that said she was done being a mom."

His words did not compute and she gaped at him, trying to make sense of what he'd confessed. He was such a devoted father to that little boy, how on earth could he have only just met him?

"I'm sorry, what?" she asked, hoping to get clarification that would help her reconcile the father-and-son duo with whom she'd recently spent the day with the picture Aiden's words painted.

"Look, I…" Aiden paused, as if considering how much to reveal. "Jamie is the result of a one-night stand. I didn't see her at all between the next morning and the custody hearing. We haven't seen or heard from her since. As best as I know, she's trying to make her way out in California. She wants to be an *actress*."

The way he spit out the word *actress* cleared

up a lot for Stella. It didn't take a genius to see why he was so against being on camera and why he'd hated her on sight. His past experience told him that actresses weren't to be trusted. Maybe she was helping him to see that she and his ex were not the same, but she imagined the mistrust might flare up again when she least expected it.

This knowledge added another reason to the growing list of why Stella should keep this relationship squarely in the pretend category. If only for her own self-preservation, she needed to remember that Aiden would never consider her for anything long-term due to his prejudice against actresses. Well, at least she knew where she stood in his esteem and would be going in with her eyes wide open if they did progress to anything more than an on-screen romance.

And if they did, it could only be temporary. A fling, at best.

After the way things had ended with Oliver, though, she was hardly planning to settle down. A temporary fling, augmented by some on-camera flirting, suited her just fine.

"Any woman who could walk away from that sweet boy is a fool."

And doubly so for walking away from his father.

Aiden hated the damper he'd put on their evening by bringing up Britney. He could never forgive her for what she'd put Jamie through. Such a sweet, innocent child and she'd treated him like a disposable plate—tossed in the trash when his usefulness to her ended.

As a newborn, Jamie had drawn a lot of attention her direction. Everyone wanted to see the new baby and it had fed her desire to be in the spotlight. From what Aiden had been able to gather, Britney had lost all interest in the child about the time he learned to walk. That's when the neglect had begun but it had taken another year before she dropped him off at St. Matthew's with the front desk nurse, a diaper bag and a note basically saying, "Tag, you're it, Daddy."

Jamie had been underweight, and still in clothes a size too small. The boy's innocent but terrified gaze had drawn him in. Even before the reality of Jamie being his son had settled over him, a fierce protectiveness for the child had filled Aiden's soul. After giving the boy a thorough checkup, Aiden had begun the legal nightmare of trying to gain custody of his son.

Only the fact that his own parents were already registered foster parents had allowed Jamie to stay with them. Aiden had been forced to move back into his old bedroom for a while to be under the same roof as his son until the DNA tests could come back proving what Aiden already knew in his heart—Jamie was truly his son.

Even now, months later, the mere mention of Britney soured his mood and he didn't see that changing in the future. Forgiving her might take longer than a lifetime. It certainly wouldn't be anytime soon.

"That must have been very hard on Jamie. And you, as well." Stella reached out and smoothed her fingers over his. "He seems to be quite healthy now."

Aiden entwined his fingers with Stella's and looked over at her. While her words were meant to be reassuring, they only brought back how far Jamie had come. "He didn't speak at all for the first month that we had him. Wouldn't say if he was hungry or cold. He didn't laugh. Barely smiled. All we could get was him nodding for yes and shaking his head for no."

"It must have been hard to see him that way." Stella bit her lip like she wanted to ask more but wasn't sure the question would be well received.

"Ask what you like," Aiden offered cautiously, "but I reserve the right to limit my response if it's too painful to discuss."

Things like how he'd needed to have his son checked for more than just mental and physical neglect was a topic he refused to discuss. It had taken all he had to say the words to the pediatrician to have the exams done to be sure. Words he hoped he'd never have to utter again. Thankfully, it had proven to be "only" neglect and Jamie's exams had revealed no physical abuse. The neglect had caused mental trauma, for certain, but Aiden and the team of doctors he'd hired were confident that with time, Jamie would fully recover.

"I started to ask if you'd had him to see a psychiatrist, but then I realized I already knew the answer. You're a physician. Of course you've taken him to every specialist who might help."

Aiden nodded. "Psychiatrists, play therapy, speech therapy, developmental pediatricians, you name it. He's still under the care of several different therapists and specialists, actually. He's slowly opening up, but it's been a gradual process."

"I'm sure he will once he's learned that he's safe." Shadows haunted Stella's eyes. The intensity of her next words made him reconsider all that he knew about Stella Allen. "In my experience, safety makes all the difference."

"Now I'm the one with questions."

"It's nothing compared to what you and sweet Jamie have been through," Stella whispered. "Let's leave it, as I've had my fair share of times where I didn't feel safe. I don't want to unpack all that tonight. Weren't we going to ice skate?"

"I overshared on the first fake date." Aiden grimaced. The word fake burned like a lie on his tongue. "Does that mean a second fake date is out of the question?"

"You were the one who said we should get to know one another more." Stella's hand was soft as it trailed along his jawline. "I think the evening is still redeemable. But perhaps we should stick to lighter fare for the rest of the evening."

Her touch reignited the blaze between them. The look on her face made him want to take her in his arms, to kiss her until the bright morning light crept over the multistory buildings surrounding them. He hadn't made out in a car with a girl since he was in college.

Stella deserved more than that. So, instead of reclining the seat and pulling her across the console, he put the car back in Drive.

"The skating rink is a few blocks away."

CHAPTER ELEVEN

HAVING HAD LITTLE real experience with relationships that involved ex drama, Stella wasn't sure how to respond to all that Aiden had just disclosed. Her heart ached for all that little Jamie's mother had put him through, and Aiden, as well. She wanted to pull him close and soothe his hurts away, but that would be inappropriate. Unless they actually were starting something up…

Tonight revealed a few of her inadequacies in the dating world though. This fake relationship was feeling all too real. And a bit beyond her comfort level. She'd dated, of course, but something about Aiden, about the connection they shared, felt different. Comforting his hurts involved more than physical care. She'd have to ease the mental angst his past had wrought on his ability to trust, and that would take time. Getting seriously involved with a single dad meant not only being in a relationship with him, but also with the child. And given that she'd sworn off motherhood, that was another red flag on the still growing list of why she shouldn't get close to Aiden Cook.

"My parents used to bring me here every winter," Aiden told her as they pulled up to the rink.

Large lights surrounded the oval-shaped expanse of ice and created a sparkle effect. Stella gasped. "Aiden, it's simply magical! How amazing that you were able to come here each winter!"

"It really was." Aiden's face lit up at the happiness of his memories. "We'd skate for hours and drink so much hot chocolate that I'd be up half the night with a sugar rush. My hands and feet would be numb from the cold, but my heart and soul were warm from all the laughter."

"That sounds perfect." Stella couldn't quite keep the longing from her voice. She couldn't imagine her mum on ice skates for even an hour. The only time her parents had taken her skating as a child had been on camera and her mum had spent most of the time sitting on a bench bragging about Stella to the other mums.

Her dad had been happy out on the ice, but not enough to take her frequently.

Aiden rented them some skates and while they were lacing them up, he asked, "So, what sort of activities did you and your parents do? Besides the trivia shows and television programs, I mean."

Stella snorted, covering her nose at the very unladylike sound that had just come out of her. "You mean besides what was videoed for *Stay Smart with Stella*? Nearly everything had to have an educational component—my mum was adamant about that. Ice skating wasn't educational. Sports, also a no-go. We played quite a few board games and read a lot."

"Educational and fun don't always align."

"Nor do they need to," Stella agreed. Her mum had been determined to keep education as a top priority for Stella, only coming second to the determination to keep their family in the spotlight, and sometimes Stella thought she had missed out on a lot of typical childhood things as a result.

She stood on the blades, gingerly finding her balance. "I don't want to give the impression that I have bad parents. I'm sure they did what they thought was best for me—they just didn't consider the alternatives. They didn't consider my personality in the decision."

Aiden stood next to her, showing far more confidence on the ice than Stella could muster. "Which parts were not to your liking? The board games or the reading?"

"I quite like board games, actually, and I read at least a book a week. I wasn't a fan of having the camera follow my every move." She'd complied with it in effort to please her parents, trying to win a scrap of praise from her mum in particular.

Aiden raised a brow. "And yet you're currently filming another program. As an adult, you don't have to do television anymore if you don't enjoy it."

Stella sighed. His words seemed so judgmental. How could she best phrase it so that Aiden could properly understand her motivations?

"That is true, yes. But this particular program is quite dear to my heart." Television had long since lost the glitter of excitement for her and had become something of a rather expected obligation. She could never truly explain how being on television had bought her a somewhat peaceful relationship with her mum, how it had helped provide an income for her family to supplement their retirement or that she had no idea how to step away without ruining that fragile equilibrium between herself and her mum. So, she smiled at him before changing the subject rather abruptly. "Race you to the other side."

She pushed off and did her best to cross the ice before Aiden. Wobbling a bit, she gained speed. The unmistakable sound of a blade on ice followed her and Aiden passed her in seconds.

He turned and slowed his pace, skating backward just a few feet ahead of her. The cold put some color in his cheeks that made him even more irresistible. He grinned broadly. "Am I racing a surgeon or a sloth?"

"Remember who won the race between the tortoise and the hare?" she teased right back. "Initial speed isn't everything."

He changed directions again, moving toward her with a slow deliberateness. Skating right up to her, he put his hands at her waist and pulled her close. "I can think of a few other activities where slow can be a good thing."

"So much for the ice being as good as a cold shower," Stella breathed more than said as she found herself pressed tightly against Aiden's broad chest. They were on the verge of melting this ice. Were fake dates allowed to be this hot?

Nothing permanent could come of it, but they were also both consenting adults. Why were they denying themselves what they both so clearly wanted?

She threw caution to the wind, wrapped her arms around his neck and kissed him. His lips were hot on hers, contrasting with the brisk air surrounding them. The contrast only made the kiss seem, oh, so much hotter. Her fingers tangled in his thick hair, and when she sighed in contentment, Aiden deepened the kiss.

The sounds of downtown Toronto faded as Aiden's lips moved over hers. All that mattered in that moment was the feeling of his arms around her and the taste of his tongue as it slid along hers.

"Watch out!" someone shouted.

Aiden lifted his head away from hers, and Stella immediately began scanning for potential danger.

She watched in horror as a teen girl skated

straight into a young couple, knocking them both over like pins at a bowling alley. They separated like a seven-ten split.

The couple cautiously got back to their feet, dusting the ice shavings from their clothing. Shaken, but seemingly physically fine, they made their way back to each other.

Unfortunately, the teen girl who had careened into them was not so lucky.

One glance at the kid who'd crashed into the couple galvanized Aiden into action. "Her leg is broken. Someone call 911!"

"Are you…?" Stella called after him as he skated over to the girl's side. "Well, I was going to ask if you were sure, but now I see that you're right."

He crouched down next to the girl. "Your leg is broken. Try not to move too much, okay?"

She cried out, "It really hurts."

"I know it does." He pulled his gloves off and tucked them into one of his pockets. "I'm a doctor over at St. Matthew's Hospital. I work in the emergency department. Is it okay if I take a look?"

She nodded.

Aiden gently put his hands on the teen's leg. She cried out as he palpated her leg. "Feels like you've fractured your tibia. Can't let you put any weight on this leg until you get X-rays, but it looks like you'll be spending the next several weeks with a cast."

Tears welled up in the teen's eyes. "I don't want to be in a cast over Christmas!"

Stella appeared next. "I had my arm casted at Christmas once. Everyone drew little Christmas trees and ornaments across it. It was quite festive."

"I think she's got a tibial fracture," Aiden told her. "This is my friend Stella. She's actually an orthopedic surgeon. Do you mind if she takes a look?"

The teen shook her head.

"I'll be gentle," Stella assured her. Her face was still and emotionless as she carefully examined the girl's leg. "I'd say that's definitely broken. The good news is that it's not an open fracture as it didn't pierce the skin. Definitely displaced though."

"Did you bump your head at all?" Aiden asked, using the flashlight on his phone to check her eyes.

"No." She sniffed. "Only my leg hurts."

"Pupils are equal and reactive to light. Very good." Aiden turned and carefully unlaced the girl's skate. "Stella, could you help immobilize while I get this skate off?"

Stella placed a hand on either side of the break and Aiden gingerly slid the skate off the girl's foot.

"Pulse is strong," he told Stella. That was a good sign. In the distance, he could hear the wail of the ambulance. The girl was still talking, pulse was good and she had no symptoms of concussion. All postive news.

They waited with her for the ambulance to arrive and Aiden gave the paramedics the vitals and his preliminary diagnosis. Stella skated up beside him as the stretcher rolled toward the ambulance.

"It's a good thing I geek out over broken bones," Stella said, leaning her head against his shoulder. "First kisses are meant to bring fireworks, not fractures."

"What can I say—I'm an overachiever." Aiden roared with laughter. "This is really shaping up to be the worst first date in history. Or are we jinxed and accidents follow us around?"

"It's not been all bad. Wasn't there a promise of hot chocolate?" She smiled up at him. "Load it with extra marshmallows and I might let you have a second kiss a bit later."

"Bribing me for chocolate already, are you?"

"Is it working?" Her eyes sparkled in the twilight.

"Maybe," he said as he skated away toward the snack stand.

More than maybe.

He paid for two hot chocolates, one with extra marshmallows as requested. What was he doing? He couldn't see a transatlantic relationship working in the long-term, and he had Jamie to consider. But maybe they could enjoy each other until she left at Christmas.

When he turned to skate back to Stella, he saw she was standing in the midst of a group of people. A few he recognized from the hospital. A radiant smile brightened her face.

He skated over slowly and held out her hot chocolate without saying a word. If he were being honest with himself, he was afraid that whatever words came out of his mouth would be sappy or cheesy. Instead, he stood next to her silently and waited for her to say something. When he was around Stella he felt sixteen again—awkward and full of unfamiliar feelings. This woman brought up scary amounts of emotions within him. Eventually, maybe, he'd learn to get a better control over it.

"Aiden, you remember Tyler and Gemma, right? And do you know Ben? He works in oncology at St. Matthew's and guess what? He managed to catch *everything* on film. I was just telling him that I'd love to use some of the footage he captured. I'll have to clear it with Martin, of course, but I think it would be amazing if I could add some clips showing that even when off duty, medical professionals will still step up and take charge. Don't you?" She held the hot chocolate up and let the heat waft over her face. "Mmm...this smells delicious, thank you."

"You're welcome," he finally muttered.

Tyler and Gemma made their excuses and skated away hand in hand, looking very much in love. Ben also said his goodbyes, and Stella waved him away with a smile and a promise to follow up with him about using his footage.

She turned back to Aiden with a question in her eyes that he'd really hoped to avoid.

She pressed the issue. "Wanna tell me what changed you from Flirty Frank to Grumpy Gus in just a few moments?"

He shook his head. "It's nothing."

Stella's brows raised. "I'm not sure I agree."

"So, do you really think the footage Ben got will be usable for the program?" Deliberately, he changed the subject, hoping beyond hope that Stella would go along with it.

She stared at him over the rim of her cup, her eyes searching his. The intelligent way she searched his face said she had calculated and came up with exactly the right answer.

He swallowed hard and resisted the urge to shift and spill his guts like a wayward child. What was this woman's sway over him? How could he tell her that seeing her smile like that made him want to do whatever it took to keep her smiling? It was their first date, and it was supposed to be fake. That was a bit too far and he needed to cool it down some.

"I'm hopeful," she said cautiously. "He caught some really good angles. I'd have to get permission from the girl's family, but it would go a long way toward satisfying Martin's request for me to have an onscreen romance, as Ben caught us kissing and working together to keep her calm."

Tension invaded his muscles. Ben had nabbed their first kiss on camera and now it would be broadcast to an undefined number of viewers. He had expected that part of their relationship would be on film, accepted it even, but he'd thought tonight was private. Life on camera would take some adjustment, knowing that everyone would be able to see everything.

He wasn't sure he wanted that. As a very reserved person, the invasion of privacy tonight rankled. He hadn't considered just how invasive the cameras would be.

Did Stella ever have any true privacy? How did anyone ever come to terms with that?

He couldn't help but wonder how Jamie would react if someone pointed a camera at him. Aiden had just gotten his son into the hospital day care, so there was a slight chance Jamie could be captured on film. Would seeing Jamie on screen bring Britney back out of the woodwork so that she could try to exploit his connection to Stella? The answer to that seemed readily apparent. She'd tossed Jamie aside when he was of no use to her, but Aiden didn't think for a minute that she'd stay away if she saw her son on screen.

She'd want him back.

He could not put his son at risk.

"I think I should take you home now."

"Aiden, what's wrong?" Stella reached toward him but he shrugged off her touch and skated toward the bench where they'd left their shoes.

Aiden's sudden reluctance to talk bothered Stella a lot more than she wanted to let on. He made the barest minimum of small talk as they drove back to her place. But more than his silence, the emotions playing out across his face concerned her. She could see he was struggling with something. Whatever it was, he wasn't yet willing to share.

When they reached her apartment, Aiden got out of the car. What was he doing? He didn't want to talk, but he thought he should walk her in? Stella couldn't understand him.

"Are you going to talk to me or just keep peeking at me like you're afraid I might bite?"

Stella was startled, embarrassed that he'd

caught her tentative glances. Wrapping her arms around herself, she said, "You don't have to walk me in."

"Yes, I do." He jabbed at the button for the elevator.

She stepped into the elevator the minute the doors opened. His hot-and-cold behavior left her a little hesitant. Aiden Cook had something of substance about him that drew her in though, even when he tried to push her away. "I've spent the whole trip here in thought, wondering exactly where things went astray."

Aiden winced. "I deserve that. I've been trying to figure out what I need to say too, but the words aren't coming easily."

"Indeed." Stella raised a brow at him. "I've drawn my own conclusions, of course. If I'm wrong, do feel free to correct me. I think you had a bit of a panic over finding out our first kiss was on camera."

"Kissing on camera was part of it, yes." He let out a shaky breath. "I'm not sure I want my private moments filmed and plastered across the internet."

"I can remove any parts that contain or mention you." Dread seeped into her bones. Martin was going to implode when she snatched the budding romance from his wrinkly fingertips.

"No." Aiden's vehement denial sparked the tiniest flame of hope.

"No?"

"I keep my word, Stella." He took her hand in his. "I was struggling to come to terms with it all. I don't want to promise that I'm one-hundred-percent sorted, but I'm doing my best. No more disappearing act. No more silent treatment."

"Your best is all I can ask," Stella said with a small smile. Prudence demanded that she guard her heart when with Aiden though. She had only a month left in Toronto and what would happen then?

She was hardly about to give up her career for a man she'd only just met, and she was sure he'd be unwilling to give up his and uproot his son for her. Real emotion couldn't be risked. A holiday fling was all this could ever be.

"Was there more than that?" she asked, sensing that he was holding something back.

"It hit me that a certain someone might try to use the connection to you to further her own career."

"Jamie's mum, you mean." Stella hadn't considered that Jamie's mum might come back into the picture. Aiden's swift retreat made so much sense after that realization. If that's where his mind had gone, she couldn't blame him for needing a bit of space. He'd had to fight so hard for his son, and if he thought being with her could put that in jeopardy, it wasn't a surprise that he withdrew. "Hmm… I hadn't thought of that possibility," she admitted.

Aiden had been adamant that Jamie's mum was gone for good, but if she wanted to be involved in the television world, she might do anything to give herself a leg up. Stella had seen a lot of people do a lot of sketchy things for a few moments of fame.

"I hadn't until just a bit ago either. I owe you an apology for the way I reacted. It wasn't very adult of me, and I can only tell you that I'm sorry and I'll try to do better going forward. Opening up is hard for me." Aiden grimaced.

"What do you think she might do?" Stella chewed her lower lip in thought.

Aiden grunted. "Well, from what I was able to learn, she used to take him on set for the extra attention. She might worm her way back into Jamie's life, trying to get close to you and the people you know."

"I see." Stella looked at him closely. From the worry lines around his eyes to the grim set of his mouth, his concern marred his face.

"I hate that she's still affecting my life like this. I'd hoped that when the custody issue was settled she'd be out of my life for good. The thought that she might find a crack that she could exploit to weasel back in, that she might hurt Jamie again… I like you, Stella. A lot. It's just—"

"You aren't the only one to consider," she interrupted.

"Exactly."

"Well, I'll do my best to keep Jamie and any mention of him off camera." She fumbled with her keys to unlock the door. "And she can hardly use a single fake date against you, so I don't think you should worry."

"Does this really feel fake to you?" Aiden moved closer, pinning her to the door with his frame. She sucked in a sharp breath at his sudden nearness. Her hands came up to clutch at his muscular shoulders just before he settled his mouth over hers. The nervous flutter in the pit of her stomach disappeared as his tongue flicked along the edge of her lower lip, tempting her to open her mouth so that he could deepen the kiss.

And man, could he kiss. Flames of desire started at her lips and radiated out until every inch of her body had sparked alive. She returned his attentions with equal fervor.

He broke away, gasping for air. Pressing his forehead to hers, his voice shook when he said, “That definitely wasn’t fake.”

Stella’s cheeks were pink and her lips had the swollen appeal of having just been thoroughly kissed. One of her hands still clutched at his shirt, keeping him close.

Even though she wasn’t the sort of woman he’d normally consider his type, Stella was beautiful. The spattering of freckles across her nose made her more approachable. And her curves? Curves like Stella’s were what dreams were made from. She was smart and sassy… and leaving in little more than a month.

A small smile tugged at her lips. “No, I dare say it wasn’t fake.”

"So, where does that leave us when you aren't staying in Canada? Have fun while it lasts?" He brushed a lock of hair away from her face. He searched for emotion in her expression. While he'd love nothing more than to go inside and take Stella to bed, he found himself allowing her to set the pace. Maybe they could just have some fun together, appreciate each other with no pressure to make it permanent.

"Hmm…" Stella's noncommittal sound gave no indication as to whether she was considering his question or not.

He bit back the urge to repeat himself. Instead, he suggested, "We could take this conversation inside."

She smirked at him. "You'd enjoy that, wouldn't you?"

Leaning in, he whispered in her ear, "I'd make sure you enjoyed it too."

"You know, I've never quite understood the joy in party planning. Decor and menus have never been all that exciting for me."

By changing the subject to the Christmas party, she threw a roadblock into the tension that had been building between them. He recognized the tactic.

Easing back, he gave her a little more space. But he couldn't keep the double entendre from creeping into his words. "Maybe you've been party planning with the wrong people?"

"Oh, is that the problem?" She raised a perfectly sculpted brow at him, clearly picking up the second meaning behind his words. "And I suppose you're the right man for the job?"

"Only one way to find out," he teased. He didn't press forward for another kiss though, as he sensed Stella wasn't ready. They only had weeks until she went back to the UK, but if he pushed too much, she might shut down entirely. He kept his tone light and flirty when he made his next pitch. "Let me take you to the Winter Festival of Lights this weekend."

"Christmas lights?" She looked skeptical.

"Niagara Falls at Christmas is an experience you can't miss while you're here." She clearly needed more persuading, so he brought up the party they were planning. "It'll be perfect research for the party decor. We can spend the evening surrounded by the Christmas spirit. What could be more exciting and inspiring than that?"

"Another fake date?"

Lifting one shoulder, he gave a casual shrug. "Why put a label on it?"

Her lips pursed together briefly before she blurted out a question. "And what of your concerns about your son and your ex?"

Aiden swallowed hard. "If there's no camera to film our every move, then there's no need for Britney to find out."

"So, a secret fake date?" Her lips twitched like she might be fighting back a smile.

"A secret fake date disguised as a research trip," he said with a grin.

"Fine. I suppose I'll go."

"Yes!" He pumped his arm in victory. "I should go, before we have any other clandestine activities to disguise."

Stella surprised him by rising up and brushing her lips across his. "Then I'll just say good night."

He waited until the lock clicked audibly as she locked the door behind her before he walked away. Was he getting in too deep with her? With every touch, every kiss, his feelings for Stella grew stronger. This was not supposed to turn into anything real. The line he was toeing was a fine one. If he didn't maintain his balance, Stella or Jamie might be hurt. It was a real risk, so he'd have to proceed with caution.

The best solution would be to stay away from Stella Allen.

If only she didn't draw him in like a tractor beam, he might be able to do that.

CHAPTER TWELVE

STELLA FOUND HERSELF strolling at Aiden's side on a crisp winter night. The trip down to Niagara Falls had been quite fun. They'd had a lot of lively conversations in the car on the way. She kept sneaking glances at him as they walked through the Christmas light display. He looked so carefree when he was with his son. The Aiden with her now was certainly not the grumpy man she'd met at the airport, but he wasn't the sharp professional from the hospital either. This Aiden was the version she liked the best. This Aiden smiled a lot. He joked, and he teased.

Stella's eyes flicked down toward Jamie. Once again, Aiden had surprised her by bringing his son along for the evening. She'd managed to hide it a bit better this time, avoiding another reappearance of defensive Aiden. And she honestly didn't mind that he'd brought his son the first time; it had merely been unexpected.

A crisp breeze blew past them, ruffling their clothing. Aiden bent and adjusted Jamie's hat, tugging it down closer around the boy's ears. "It's a little chilly out tonight, but I promised Jamie that we'd come see the Christmas lights—even though he's going to be up way past his bedtime."

Jamie gave a tiny little grin at the playful tone in Aiden's voice.

"Normally he'd be in bed soon, but it's Christmas lights. You can only see those for such a limited time. So, we struck a bargain that he'd be allowed to stay up tonight if he napped today. So, what do you think? Are you finding a bit of Christmas spirit?"

"Of course." She wrapped a gloved hand around his biceps. Maybe if she moved a little closer she could share a bit of his body heat. "I'm so happy to have been invited, even if it is quite cold."

"I'm glad you came too." He tossed a look her way that made her feel like they were standing in Death Valley midsummer rather than the middle of a Canadian winter.

Trying for a distraction from the heat building in her core, Stella pointed at the animatronic reindeer that was moving off to their left. “Look at Rudolph! Jamie, what’s your favorite reindeer?”

“Wudolph,” Jamie answered, exactly as she expected.

“Mine too,” she said conspiratorially. She’d always loved the reindeer with the red nose and the courage to stand out too. “Which one do you think is Daddy’s favorite? I think it’s Dasher.”

Jamie nodded solemnly in agreement. Even surrounded by animatronic animals and thousands of twinkling lights, it was hard to get a smile from the little boy. She wanted to start singing a Christmas carol, maybe in a funny voice, to see if she could pull a laugh from Jamie.

Walking along the marked path was a bit like walking through a winter wonderland. Between the slight crunch of snow beneath their feet and the soft flurries falling around them, the atmosphere was perfect for getting into the Christmas spirit. All it was missing were a cup of peppermint hot chocolate and some Christmas carols.

"Dasher? Really? Very funny, guys," Aiden said with a roll of his eyes. "I've always been fond of Cupid actually."

"Really?"

"Really. Cupid seems like she'd be grumpy that everyone assumed she was a romantic because of her name. I relate to the grumpy."

Stella laughed until tears ran down her face. "At least you can admit that you are a grump. I have to say, I thought you were going to be a nightmare when we first met. You had me regretting that I'd agreed to come to Toronto. Turned my impression that all Canadians were overly polite and friendly straight on its ear."

"I admit that I didn't make the best first impression." He leaned closer and her heart rate ticked up at the closeness. "But even then, we had crazy chemistry. Just a touch of our hands was enough to keep me up most of the night thinking about the what-ifs."

"Oh?" She tried not to sound too eager for his answer, but it wasn't every day that a gorgeous man confessed to thinking about you all night.

In fact, to Stella's recollection, this was the first time a man had ever made such a confession to her. She found herself comparing Aiden to the other guys she'd dated, but there was no real comparison. He was the kind of man every woman hoped to find.

That comparison led her to wondering what else was different between her life in Toronto and her life back in the UK. Her career, obviously, was on a path she was happy with back home. Although, other than a few snotty people, the staff at St. Matthew's Hospital had been extremely welcoming. She'd been asked to drinks more in the month of November than the past six at the Royal Kensington Hospital. Okay, so the bar had been quite low on that and she'd only been asked once, by Gemma, but Stella still had to count that as a pro for Toronto.

Of course, her personal life back home was nothing to brag about. She had been longing for the connection of close friends for a while, but none had materialized. She thought if she had more time in Canada that Gemma might become that close friend she'd always felt was missing from her life. And her abysmal dating life would be watched with abject horror if it were to be filmed.

She paused.

How was it that in a month she had a more satisfying social life in Toronto than she'd managed to build in nearly a year in London? And this Christmas was shaping up to be the best one she'd had in years. She hadn't done multiple Christmas activities in the same holiday season in longer than she could remember.

"You okay?" Aiden questioned. They paused to look at a brightly lit two-story-high fountain. "Considering all the festivity surrounding us, you seem a bit down."

"Just thinking."

"Doesn't seem like good thoughts?"

"Hmm... Neither good nor bad, merely confusing." Stella leaned her head against his shoulder. "Simply thinking of how different my life is here versus my life in London."

Slipping an arm around her waist, Aiden pulled her in close. "Do I dare hope that there's at least one thing you like better here?"

She tiptoed to brush a kiss across his lips, mindful of Jamie being on his opposite hip. "I can think of at least two right now."

Aiden smiled before kissing her again. His kiss was far less chaste than the one she'd just bestowed on him. "We are growing pretty fond of you too, Stella."

"My turn kiss Stella," Jamie insisted. He puckered up his little lips and leaned in to smack a kiss on Stella's cheek.

Her heart melted at the little boy's actions. "Oh, my heart, you are the most adorable creature in existence," she cooed.

"Shall we continue on? There's a lot left to see here."

They continued on, walking through a tunnel of light loops. The colors of the lights changed as they continued to walk, and Jamie was so fascinated that they had to circle back and go again. The lightwork gave the impression of a passage through a portal.

"I wonder if we could set up something similar at the party, maybe for the kids to go through to get to the cookie station?"

"I think that would be brilliant." Aiden grinned. "I know at least one little one who might be more interested in that than he would be in the cookies."

Pointing ahead, and whispering in Jamie's

ear, Aiden convinced his son to go on and see more of the Winter Festival of Lights when he wanted to go through the light passage once more. Before long, they came up on what Aiden must have told Jamie about, because the boy squealed with excitement.

A warmth she'd never felt came over her when she saw the pure joy on Jamie's face. He ran ahead to a giant keyboard with music notes on the wall behind it. His giggles filled the air as he ran from one end to the other and the lights changed colors with his steps. Each step played a musical note.

"He laughed," Aiden breathed more than said. He pulled her into his arms and hugged her tightly. "Did you hear? He actually laughed."

"I heard," she said back in a whisper, as if afraid speaking louder would break the spell.

They stood, looking at Jamie playing a few feet away, still wrapped in each other's arms. Stella relaxed against Aiden and he leaned his cheek against the top of her head. Nothing in Stella's life had ever felt more perfect.

"You have a lovely family," an older woman said. "Have a Merry Christmas!"

"Merry Christmas," they both murmured in return.

"I suppose we do look like a family," she said, extracting herself from Aiden's embrace. She was getting too wrapped up in the romance of the evening. She shouldn't be allowing herself to get so close to them. With every moment she spent with them, she found herself wishing circumstances were different and that she weren't leaving in a month.

Maybe she should just step away before she hurt Jamie like his own mother had done? Or gave him the same sort of long-term issues that her own mother had given her. And she certainly didn't want to provide an "in" for Britney to hurt Jamie again.

Plus, she wasn't sure she was the mothering type.

Wrapping her arms around herself, she tried to will away the ache that sat down deep in her chest.

Stella visibly withdrew after the old woman's comment about them being a family. Had it upset her that someone would think they were a couple?

Worse, was she upset that the woman might have thought she was Jamie's mom? That one dug deep and latched on. Who would be embarrassed by an adorable little boy?

He could see her struggling. Emotions were flashing across her face with unreadable speed. It had to be connected to the woman's words. They'd shared a few light kisses and she'd been content in his arms up until that moment.

"Talk to me," he said. "She upset you. What I'm not understanding is exactly how? And the reasons I'm coming up with in my head are not good."

"You're a dad."

"Yeah."

News flash, I was a dad when we met.

He searched her gaze for the relevancy to that fact. "And?"

"I'm not sure I'm cut out to be someone's mum."

Those words cut straight to his heart, piercing his soul faster than any insult or criticism ever could. The weight on his chest made it hard to breathe. Stella didn't want to be a mother. Or a stepmother, in this case.

"His mom said something very similar at the

custody hearing when she signed over rights." He picked up his son and hugged him tight, wanting to shield him from any further pain.

"Aiden—"

"No, it's better that we're honest about what this is, and what this isn't before any of us get truly attached." He sighed. "I was starting to really like you, Stella, starting to think of how we might make something work long-term despite living on separate continents, but this is one thing that I can't look past."

"I'm trying to be up-front about what I'm thinking." She reached out a hand toward him, but he stepped back out of her reach.

"What about him isn't enough?" She'd seemed to really like spending time with Jamie. Had it all been an act?

Her jaw dropped. She recovered quickly, and argued, "It's not that, Aiden. He deserves only the best."

"It's already past his bedtime—we should go see the falls and then head home."

"Aiden," she called after him, but he'd already stomped away. He stopped at the viewing platform where they could see the colorfully lit frozen Niagara Falls. Its beauty couldn't be denied, even when frustration ran through his veins unchecked.

Stella stepped up next to him. “I’ve never seen anything like that.” Awe filled her voice. “Jamie, what do you think? You like the pink waterfall?”

“Pretty,” Jamie said, not taking his eyes off the falls. “Ooh! Blue!”

The lights at the falls changed to another bright hue, casting a bluish tinge across Stella’s face. She stared out at the icy waterfall, and he thought he caught the glimpse of tears in her eyes.

Jamie yawned and reached his arms out to Stella. But Aiden couldn’t let Jamie get even more attached to her.

“Not right now, buddy,” Aiden said, denying his son’s request. He tried not to wince at the gruffness in his voice. Hugging Jamie closer, he tried to soften his refusal.

“Are you ready to go?” Stella asked quietly.

With a quick nod, he walked away. No, he came close to running. Power walking had nothing on him as he strode back to the car, eager to put any distance between himself and

Stella. How could he have put Jamie in this position again?

Stella trailed behind a bit, reaching the car after he'd secured his son in the back and closed the door.

"I don't suppose we can talk about this?" she asked as she walked up. She'd wrapped her arms around herself like she needed a hug and he wanted so much to reach out and pull her into his arms.

What was wrong with him? Why did he want to comfort someone who didn't want to be involved with him and his son?

"What's left to say, Stella? I have a kid. You don't want to be a mom."

She shook her head. "Aiden, that's not exactly what I meant."

"Isn't it?" He released a shaky breath. "What did you mean then? Because I don't see any other way I could take that."

"I'm not good at this. I've messed up every relationship I've ever started." She looked down at her feet, no longer meeting his eyes. "I don't know what to say to fix this."

"I promised earlier that I'd try to talk more. To not just shut you out when something bothers me." He swallowed hard. His resolve to keep his distance almost broke. He needed to stay strong, for Jamie. "When I touch you, I can see an amazing future stretched out in front of us."

"I can too," she whispered.

"But when you say things like thinking that you aren't cut out to be a mom, all I see is history repeating itself. All I see is another woman willing to walk away from my son to further her career." He should have known better than to try to get involved with another actress.

"Aiden, I—"

He cut her off, not wanting to hear any excuses. "Get in the car so I can drive you home."

They made the car ride to her apartment in silence. The drive back seemed far longer than the drive there had. But he couldn't think of a single thing to say that wouldn't be the start of a fight he didn't want to have in front of his son. When he turned into the parking garage, she glanced back at Jamie.

"He's asleep, so there's no need for you to get out of the car to walk me up."

After pulling up next to the elevator, he

waited for her to get out. He paused until she stepped inside and the elevator doors closed, taking her out of his sight. Even though he was angry with her, he needed to be sure she was safely in her building before he drove away.

How could she dismiss his son so easily? Why did women find his little boy so unlovable? Was that a genetic trait? His own birth mother had abandoned him as a child too. He'd been lucky and had been adopted by the Cooks who were the best people he'd ever known. But the question had always lingered in his mind: *Why did my parents not want me?*

From the moment he'd read the simple note that Britney had left with Jamie, he'd vowed to be the very best father he could be. He'd do all that was within his power to make sure Jamie never felt the sting of paternal rejection. Britney had walked away from their one night together without a backward glance, a fact that had never bothered him until he learned she'd given birth to his son.

By the time he reached home, he'd worked himself into a frenzy about the evening. He'd never wanted a woman to stick around before, but now, ironically, the one he wanted didn't want him. His anger with Stella for rejecting his son had spilled over into anger at himself, as well. The fact that her confession bothered him so much told him a lot: he was falling for her.

He carried Jamie into the house, still half asleep.

His mom was there to pass judgement before he'd closed the door behind them. "You look upset."

"I'm fine." He really didn't want to get into it with her tonight. He loved her, but she was one of the most stubborn people he knew and he wasn't sure he had it in him tonight to handle her interrogation without breaking.

She tilted her head and he could practically see the gears turning in her mind. "Jamie, dear, how were the Christmas lights?"

His son ratted him out. "Daddy mad with Stella."

"Traitor," he muttered under his breath. His own son had thrown him straight under the bus.

"Oh, Daddy's mad at Stella, is he?" She took his son out of his arms. "You want Grandma to get you ready for bed while grumpy ol' Daddy takes a shower and calms down?"

Jamie nodded, and his mom headed for the stairs with Jamie in her arms. He couldn't hear the words she whispered, but Aiden was sure his mother was promising things to Jamie that spoiled him rotten.

"So why does your son think you're mad at a woman?" his dad asked from the doorway behind him.

"Leave it alone, Dad," he said without turning.

"Jamie likes her, you know." His father came fully out of his office. "He's been talking about her nonstop since you went to the christmas market together."

"Jamie doesn't really know her," Aiden growled.

"And you do?"

"I know enough!" He ran his hands through his hair. "She doesn't want kids. She as good as said."

"Hmm…" His dad looked thoughtful. "Not wanting children isn't a defect."

"I know that." And he did. Truly.

"Then you're not upset with Stella, are you?"

Aiden pinched the bridge of his nose. "No, I'm mad at myself for getting involved with someone who doesn't want kids."

"I didn't want kids at first either. Your mom wore me down. I only gave in because it made her happy, but once you came into my life, I found I'd never wanted anything more. I didn't want to be a dad until about five minutes after I became one."

"She said she's not cut out to be a mom." Aiden tried harder to explain to his dad why Stella wasn't an option. "How much clearer could she be?"

"I've only got one question for you, son." His dad paused for effect. "How long was it after you met Jamie before you decided that you *were* cut out to be a dad? Because I seem to recall a similar sentiment coming from you in those early days."

Chewing on his dad's words, Aiden showered and went to bed. Even as he lay there, wide awake, the words bounced around in his head. He'd never known that his dad had been reluctant to have children.

He'd never not wanted Jamie though. He'd been completely taken with that little boy from day one. Had he questioned his ability to be what the child needed? Well, sure. But what parent hadn't questioned themselves at some point along the way? Never once had he considered walking away though.

Not even for a second.

If he were being brutally honest though, he'd never pictured himself as a family man before he suddenly became a father. Kids hadn't been high on his priority list, but once he had a son, it became his top priority. It hadn't taken long for him to realize that being someone's dad was a role he was meant to play.

In certain situations, emotions and instinct showed a man who he was meant to be. Having his son placed in his arms told him he was meant to be a father. The pain he felt at Stella's rejection told him he was meant to spend his life with her.

Sleep eluded him as he let his mind drift to what could have been with Stella. When he rolled over to check the time it was two in the morning. and the notification light on his phone flashed. He had two messages from Stella.

The first read:

I didn't mean to imply that your son wasn't perfect in any way. I think he's the most perfect child I've ever met. Me, though, I'm so far from perfect that I blew an otherwise perfect evening. He is enough. It's me that's lacking.

The second simply said:

I've an IQ of one hundred and sixty. You'd think I'd know a few synonyms for perfect.

He couldn't stop the snort of amusement at the last message.

If Jamie was perfect though, why couldn't she envision herself in his life? Unlike himself, Stella didn't have an obligation to be in Jamie's life. It would be a choice for her.

Did his dad have a point about giving her time? Or would giving her time just prolong the inevitable heartache when she boarded the plane back to her life without them?

CHAPTER THIRTEEN

"ST. MATTHEW'S DAY CARE," a frazzled voice on the other end of the call answered.

"This is Dr. Stella Allen. I received a page for this number, but I'm not quite sure why."

"Oh, thank goodness." The woman's sigh of relief was audible. "Could you please come down to the day care? We're on the first level, just behind the administration wing."

"Could I ask why?"

"It's best explained in person." The line went dead.

Curiosity piqued, Stella made her way downstairs. Why would an orthopedic surgeon be called to the hospital's crèche? Surely if any of the children were injured, they'd send them over to Emergency. Or call a trauma doctor.

She buzzed the intercom at the entrance and when she gave her name, the lock clicked open. Hesitantly, she made her way inside. Children played in various parts of the room, some quietly, some not so quietly.

"Are you Stella?" One of the day care workers asked as she walked up to Stella.

"I am." Stella couldn't see anyone hurt, no reason for her to have been called. Her confusion rose.

"Follow me," the young woman said, turning and heading toward the back. When she opened a door, the faint sounds of crying met Stella's ears.

"Is one of the children injured?" Stella picked up her pace. She had no supplies down here. How was she to handle an emergency? She took a deep breath and calmed that anxiety. She'd have to make do.

When she stepped through the door though, she saw only one child—Jamie. He sat slapping at the hands of the poor childcare provider who was trying to soothe his tears.

"Jamie, what's wrong?" She hurried to his side and sat next to him. While her instinct was to pull him into her arms and cradle him until the crying subsided, she didn't want to upset him further if he didn't want to be touched.

"Stella!" He shouted her name and jumped

into her lap. He buried his face against her throat and mumbled something she didn't understand. His breathing came in great hitching breaths as he tried to stop sobbing.

"What happened here?" she asked, trying to keep the anger and accusation out of her voice, although in that moment she wanted to shout at them all for upsetting Jamie.

The young woman who'd shown her in shrugged. "He was playing out there with the others and everything seemed fine. He was rolling a ball with another child, and it was like a switch flipped. He went from content to crying in a matter of seconds."

"How long was he crying?" Stella rubbed Jamie's back as he snuggled closer to her, still occasionally sobbing. Thankfully, the overall intensity of his cries began to reduce.

"A while. We tried to call Dr. Cook first, of course, but the ED is swamped. There was a multicar pileup on the freeway, it seems. Then we tried his grandmother, but she's at a doctor's appointment across town."

"And I was the next logical choice?" Stella couldn't keep the surprise out of her voice.

"When we told him that Daddy and Grandma couldn't come, he asked for you." She gave Stella a soft, telling look. "I'll leave you some privacy to calm him."

Why had she been given that look? The one that said she ought to know how to comfort Jamie. She hadn't spent nearly enough time with Jamie to understand what he liked or didn't. She rubbed his back gently and murmured the kind of soothing nonsense that she'd seen others use, and when Jamie responded favorably, she continued.

Slowly, Jamie's breathing settled into a steady pace and the occasional sobs faded. He fell asleep, his face pressed into Stella's throat and his breath tickling her skin. Rather than making her uncomfortable though, it filled Stella with a longing she'd never expected.

For years now, she'd told herself that she had no interest in being a mum. Stella had been loved, yes, but she'd never truly felt understood by her mum. There'd been a distance between them that Stella saw widening as the years passed. She wanted the distance—more than her mother did—but she needed more autonomy than her mum was willing to give.

What if she couldn't give a child what they really needed?

Jamie snuffled a bit, cuddling closer, his tiny little hand clutching at hers. Tears welled up in her eyes. He trusted her implicitly, enough to let his guard down and sleep in her arms. After everything he'd been through, he'd wanted her to comfort him. That had to mean something, didn't it?

One thing she knew—she'd been deceiving herself for years about not wanting kids in her life.

"I'm sorry it took me so long to get here," Aiden told the day care worker. "Where is he?"

"Asleep."

Aiden's heart dropped. Had Jamie cried himself to sleep again? Nausea bubbled up in his stomach at the thought of his sweet baby crying until he couldn't cry anymore. It wouldn't be the first time, but Aiden had hoped it wasn't going to happen anymore.

"They both are," she said with a smile.

"Both?"

She opened the door to the room at the back used for naps and quiet time. Over her shoulder, Aiden saw a sight he never would have expected.

Stella sat in the rocker, eyes closed, with Jamie cuddled against her chest asleep. Her cheek rested on the top of Jamie's head. Matching looks of contentment graced their faces. By all appearances, they were a natural pair.

He sighed.

"I hope you don't mind that we called Dr. Allen down. We tried your mom after we got word from the ED that you might be a while. She couldn't make it either and he was so upset. He started asking for Stella and we knew you two have been seeing each other."

We were seeing each other.

"She wasn't on the list to take him though, but we can update that if you wish," the day care worker kept talking. "He threw himself into her arms the moment she arrived and hasn't let her go since."

And she'd stayed with him.

Aiden swallowed hard at the lump of emotion clogging his throat. In the moment, he could see a future with Stella at his side. He could see her filling the maternal role in Jamie's life.

But, somehow, *she* couldn't.

Was something in her past blocking her from seeing what an amazing mom she could be? Or had he missed a key piece in her background that changed everything?

He didn't know.

What he did know was that the closer she got to Jamie, the higher the risk became that his son would get hurt.

That thought sobered him. The chinks in the wall around his heart that had softened upon seeing Jamie sleeping in her arms filled back up.

"Hey," he said softly, nudging her shoulder. He made sure to avoid touching her anywhere they might have skin to skin contact. "Stella, wake up."

"Hmm…" she murmured, voice thick with sleep. Her eyes opened and she blinked rapidly. "I must have drifted off."

"You did." He nodded down at Jamie. "I need to get him home."

"Oh, of course." She brushed a kiss on Jamie's hair before lifting him up so that Aiden could take him.

He tucked his son into his chest and turned

to go. But before he left, he couldn't help himself. He had to say something. "While I should thank you for coming down here to take care of Jamie, I can't help but worry that you've made it harder on him."

Without giving her time to respond, Aiden left the day care. He'd have to talk to them about calling for Stella. It was already going to be hard enough on Jamie when he realized that he'd never see Stella again.

CHAPTER FOURTEEN

"SOMEONE PAGED ME," Stella said as she walked into the emergency department. It had been a generic page, so she had no idea who. She had been trying unsuccessfully to squash the hope that it was Aiden and that his reason for paging her was personal for her entire walk down from ortho. She looked around hopefully, but didn't see him.

"Exam two. Mrs. Upton is back. Dr. Cook asked me to call you down here." The nurse gestured over her shoulder from where she stood on a stepladder behind the desk hanging garland along the top of the bulletin board.

Christmas decorations had started to pop up everywhere at St. Matthew's. A huge tree already took up a large portion of the waiting room, although it had yet to be decorated. Up in orthopedics, the patients had responded favorably to the festive touches and the staff were often found humming Christmas carols as they worked. Stella was loving the vibrancy of the holiday in Toronto so far.

"Mrs. Upton?" Stella's mind went into overtime, running through the details of Mrs. Upton's surgery. Everything had gone well. She'd been healing okay at her follow-up. Had there been a complication that Stella had missed during surgery or one of the exams?

She smoothed her hair and straightened her white coat before hurrying into exam two where Aiden was standing at the patient's bedside. Stella's eyes drank him in like an oasis in the desert. She hadn't seen him since the incident with Jamie in the hospital day care.

He'd ignored her calls. Read, but didn't respond to her texts. And she hadn't even caught a glimpse of him here at the hospital. He must have been determined to avoid her.

Their eyes met when he looked up at her arrival. Tension sparked between them like a live wire. Desire pooled in her abdomen. She shouldn't still want him so much after the silence, but her body reacted to a single look from him.

"Dr. Allen, how good of you to join us." The words rolled off his tongue like a rebuke. As if she had dawdled on her way down rather than arriving only minutes after she'd been paged.

"I arrived as quickly as I could, Dr. Cook," she replied with an edge to her voice. Why did his cold tone make her so hot? Two could play that icy treatment game. She'd show him that she could give as good as she received on that front.

She softened her tone when speaking to the patient though, of course. The sweet, elderly woman had done nothing to deserve the sharpness of her tongue. "Hello, Mrs. Upton, what brings you in today?"

Mrs. Upton grimaced. "I fell again."

"Oh, dear." Stella scanned her patient for visual clues of injuries. Mrs. Upton's skin looked a little washed out of color, but she seemed free of bruising or obvious damages. A glance at the monitors showed that the patient's vital signs were strong. "Can you tell me a bit about what happened?"

With a sigh, Mrs. Upton began her story. "Well, there I was at physical therapy—still at that rehab facility they sent me to, mind you—they had me up and walking along with this wheeled walker. I stumbled a bit, lost my footing and that walker just went on without me. I landed on my left hip. There was a lot of pain so the physical therapist and the doctor there thought it best I come in and let you have a look."

"It does sound prudent." Stella moved over to the computer terminal. Why had that physical therapist let her get so far ahead of them that Mrs. Upton became a fall risk? They should have been right within arm's reach so that they could support her, catch her and ease her down if she lost her balance. Incompetent. They'd be catching an earful from her this morning. "Dr. Cook, have you had new imaging done?"

"We have." His voice was tight. "The results have just popped up and I was about to review them."

Stella tapped a few keys so that she could check the patient's chart and make sure Aiden had ordered all the imaging she wanted to see done. He had.

"Okay, well, let's take a look."

Aiden looked over her shoulder, standing so close that the hint of cedar from his cologne tickled at her senses. She swallowed hard, fighting herself to focus on Mrs. Upton's imaging.

"What do you think?" he said softly, his breath warm against the back of her neck.

"Looks like everything held." Stella squeezed past Aiden, being careful not to touch him. She patted the patient's foot gently. "Looks like it's just bruising. The fracture seems to be healing well and the fall doesn't appear to have hindered that."

"I've already ordered some pain medication for you, as well," Aiden reassured the older woman. "The nurse should bring that in shortly."

He motioned for Stella to precede him out of the exam room.

"Could we chat for a moment?" she asked. "In private."

"We have nothing to say to each other."

She sighed. He wasn't going to make this easy on her at all, was he? "We still have some issues to discuss regarding the Christmas party."

With a nod, he stalked down the hall and into one of the small family rooms where the doctors took patients' loved ones to tell them bad news in private. The door clicked shut.

He crossed his arms over his chest and waited for her to speak. The shields in his eyes were fully erect, and she didn't see the charming man she'd spent time with. No, this was back to the snappy grump from the airport.

"Well?" he prompted. "If you aren't going to get on with it, I need to get back to work."

Stella closed her eyes and took a deep breath. Why had she though it was a good idea to get involved with a coworker again? "I emailed you some ideas on the party and wondered if you'd had a chance to take a look."

"No. But I'm sure whatever you've decided will be acceptable."

"Okay, so I'll just put your name down on the order for the jolly Santa strippers and the naughty Mrs. Clauses then?"

"Sure, Stella. You just tell me what you need me to take care of." He rolled his eyes. "I'm trusting you to keep it professional and work-appropriate for the rest."

"How is Jamie, by the way?" she asked. "Hopefully what happened at day care didn't upset him too badly?" She'd been worried about that for days now, and when Aiden didn't answer her calls or texts, her worries had nearly taken on a life of their own. "I tried to check in on him."

"I know."

"Is he okay?" Stella tried again. She really was concerned about the little boy. He'd been through so much and if she had added to it because of her actions, she wasn't sure how she'd handle it.

"Do you even care?" Aiden huffed. "Or are you just asking to be polite?"

"I don't think I deserve this much animosity for expressing a personal concern." Stella sighed. "I really don't want to upset your son. I hope I didn't, and I apologize if I have done so."

Aiden was more upset than she'd realized. While she'd known there was a problem, it went far deeper than first glance.

She really had some nerve! Asking about his son like she had a right to know how Jamie was. Like she cared! She'd said she wasn't cut out to be a mother, so what benefit did she gain from acting like he mattered to her?

"He told my parents we were fighting."

"You still live with your parents?"

He had to fight back a growl, but he gave her an abbreviated version of the events that had led to him moving back home. "They're licensed foster parents. They had to take Jamie in before I could gain legal custody. I moved back in with them so that I could be in the same household with my son. His psychiatrist recommended that I not uproot him again by moving out just yet."

"I see."

"Do you?" He started pacing back and forth in the small room like a caged tiger. From the door to the back wall took him only eight steps. "He's had so much upheaval already. And by introducing him to you, I brought yet another person into his life who is abandoning him."

"I didn't…"

"Didn't what? Abandon him? You cuddled him and gave him kisses and then walked away. That's exactly what you did."

Her mouth gaped open and she sank down into one of the ugly salmon-pink chairs the hospital had installed during their last reno. "I never thought…"

"Never mind." He couldn't stand to look at her anymore. Did she really not see that her actions had affected Jamie? He turned to go.

"Aiden, please wait. I know you might have watched some of my programs when you were researching me. But despite how it looked, my mother was never going to win any parenting awards in real life. I was actually a very lonely, neglected child. The bulk of my interactions with my parents occurred on camera. If the red light wasn't on, I didn't exist for them."

"Why are you telling me this?"

"I don't know how to be a mum! My decisions were all made for me for so long that I am only just now learning what I want from my own life." She went and stared out the window over the snow-covered parking lot. "I don't even know what a good mother might look like as I've never had one in my life."

"You are a fantastic doctor. You care deeply for your patients," Aiden scoffed. "And I think if you would open your eyes, you'd see that you could be an amazing mother. You've already shown more caring than Britney ever did."

She didn't turn away from the window. "After all he's been through, little Jamie deserves better than someone playing at motherhood! Children don't come with a tutorial and I have no idea where to begin."

"Parenting comes with a learning curve. A steep one. And no parent is ever perfect. The most important thing to do is to show them that they are loved." He ran a hand through his hair in frustration. "Stella, I know your parents left you with some trauma, but even if you simply do the opposite of what they did for you, you'd be a better parent than either of them ever was."

He left the room quietly, leaving her to digest all that he'd just thrown at her. He strode over to the desk. "I'm taking my break now."

He took the stairs up to the roof and stood in the cold, staring out over the Toronto skyline. Working on patients wasn't a good idea until he'd pulled himself together. What had he been thinking getting involved with another actress?

Clearly, he hadn't been using his brain, but another part of his anatomy, when he'd gotten entangled with a woman from the hospital. Particularly when her second career was in the film industry. He should have stuck with his normal routine of being alone until his physical needs got too much and then finding someone for a night to satisfy those urges. Then he didn't have to worry about finding someone who would love both him and his son.

Maybe his past had marked him as unlovable. He should focus on his son. He'd been lucky that he'd found adoptive parents like the Cooks. And despite the neglect Jamie had suffered while under Britney's care, Aiden had custody now. If he gave Jamie enough love and attention, maybe he could break the cycle.

The feelings of inadequacy that he'd struggled with his entire life resurfaced. The therapist he'd seen for a while said that his lack of self-worth when it came to relationships stemmed from his own abandonment. It had been amplified when his own son went through the same abandonment by his birth mother. Neither of them had been born to women capable of loving them.

In the past, Aiden had never let a woman get this close. He'd never wanted to. But from the undeniable chemistry whenever they touched to the intelligence that made her eyes sparkle when she talked, Stella Allen had gotten under his skin. The part that hurt the most was that he could see that Stella wasn't really as ambivalent about motherhood as she tried to tell herself. He could see what a loving, caring person she really was. Had anything he'd just said resonated with her at all?

The wind kicked up and Aiden shivered. Still, he stayed out and sucked the crisp, cold air into his lungs while trying to quiet the voice in his head that kept telling him to go find Stella, to do whatever it took to make her love him and love Jamie.

But why bother when she was leaving so soon?

CHAPTER FIFTEEN

"HEY, STELLA," GEMMA blurted out. "A really hot guy is looking for you downstairs with a camera."

Stella stopped walking and lifted her attention from the file in her hands. She blinked at her in confusion. "I beg your pardon?"

"There is a super cute British guy waiting in the lobby for your presence." Gemma rephrased and slowed her words down as if Stella hadn't heard her. It wasn't the hearing she was struggling with but the comprehension. "He has the most adorable dimples I've ever seen on an adult male."

She wasn't expecting anyone from back home to show up in Toronto. But if it was a good-looking man with a camera and dimples, she could only think of one person who fit that description, and he had no business being at St. Matthew's. "Dark hair and quite tall?" she asked.

"Got it in one. I take it you know who I'm talking about?"

"I do." Stella turned toward the stairs. "Thanks for letting me know, Gemma."

"We still need to find time to get drinks," Gemma yelled as Stella walked away.

"Absolutely," Stella called over her shoulder. She'd need a drink after she dealt with her unexpected visitor downstairs.

When she reached the crowed lobby, she saw exactly who she'd expected to find. "Oliver, to what do I owe the pleasure?"

"Stella, darling, I've missed you." Oliver took her in his arms and moved to kiss her. She turned her head just in time and his lips landed on her cheek.

"Really, Ollie, we no longer have that sort of relationship. Please, be respectful of that fact."

Oliver rolled his eyes, but released her. "Martin thought you could use my services. He said the footage that's been captured is…usable, but not very inspired. He said it needed more of a cinematic touch."

"A more cinematic touch?" With her fists clenched at her sides, Stella stared Oliver down. When the first of December had passed without Henry being replaced, Stella had thought that Martin might have changed his mind about sending someone else. Her heart sank as she realized that he'd not backed down on that at all. And of all the people he could have sent, why did it have to be the one videographer in all the world with whom she had history?

One of his shoulders lifted in a casual shrug that she'd once found attractive. At least until she learned that Oliver had as much personality as stale toast.

"Martin likes my work, and he knows I've worked with you in the past and can capture your best angles. I know how to flatter you on film, darling. I minimize those luscious curves of yours and slim you down to the perfect look." He winked at her. "Plus, I was encouraged to make the trip."

Stella shook her head in frustration. That was another reason why she and Oliver had never worked—he always wanted her to slim down so that he didn't have to film her at specific angles.

"Oliver, go home. I don't want or need your help."

"Take that up with Martin, darling. I've

checked into a hotel a few blocks down. Why don't you plan to have dinner with me this evening? We can go over what footage we still need, then you and I can get reacquainted." He reached out and took her hand. "I promise to make it worth your time."

A gasp off to the side reminded Stella that they had an audience. She snatched her hand from him quickly, but she could already see the disapproving looks on the faces of the St. Matthew's employees clustered nearby.

"You never made it worth my time when we were together, so I think I'll pass." She took another step back. "I have work to do."

"So do I," Oliver said. He swung his camera up on his shoulder. "And that's to follow you around and get some good footage for this program."

She hadn't seen Oliver since they'd broken up several months back. Her decision. Besides the utter lack of physical allure, and the dullness of his personality, Oliver wanted to grow his career in the film industry. He wanted them to take over the film world together and she wasn't sure she wanted that life. But it had been when she'd expressed her concerns about having a family that had created an unbridgeable gulf between them. She just hadn't seen a future with him.

Not like she had with Aiden.

She'd blown her chances with Aiden though. He'd been giving her a wide berth and would barely make eye contact with her. She wasn't sure how to go about repairing what she'd broken. Bones she could mend: hurt feelings, not so much.

Stella hurried back to the orthopedics floor with Oliver following right behind her. The head of the department stopped her, placing a hand on her arm, and silently asked about Oliver by flicking her gaze behind Stella to where he stood.

"Assigned to me from the director. Seems the earlier footage wasn't quite hitting the spot," she said through gritted teeth.

"Hmm..." Dr. Devlin looked at Oliver. "Stay out of my operating rooms. Be extremely careful about patient privacy. And do not get in my way."

As she walked away, Oliver snorted. "Well, she's fun."

"I quite like her actually," Stella countered.

"Give me the tour, Stella." Oliver placed his hand on her lower back. "Then we can get some dinner and get out of here."

"Can I get your signature on a few forms, Dr. Allen?" one of the nurses asked. She shoved the tablet against Stella's arm.

"Certainly," Stella said, using the distraction to once again move away from Oliver's touch.

The brief conversation with the nurse seemed snappier than usual but Stella couldn't pinpoint why. She had only had a few interactions with this particular nurse and none of them had been sour, so she wasn't sure where the animosity came from. She signed the forms quickly and handed the tablet back to the nurse.

For the rest of the day, all of her interactions went similarly. The feeling at St. Matthew's Hospital had definitely changed. The warmth and acceptance that Stella had worked so hard to earn had vanished. She'd proven herself, hadn't she? Had all her effort been for naught? Once again, Stella became an outsider and she wasn't sure why.

Based upon the number of glares, it seemed to be connected to Oliver though. Was it how he talked about her, as though she were a celebrity they should feel privileged to know? Or his insistence on filming every move? Both had to be reinforcing the staff's early belief that she was more TV personality than doctor.

And she hated it.

"Did you hear that she's already taken up with— Oh, sorry, Dr. Cook, I didn't realize you were there." The nurse and orderly who had been gossiping both flushed brightly and hurried down the hall away from him.

It was completely unnecessary. He already knew exactly who they were talking about. Rumors had reached Aiden's ears quickly about the British cameraman who was currently attached to Stella's hip. He wanted to tune out the gossips, pretend he hadn't heard the whispers of how she'd moved on already, but he was finding that impossible to do.

He hadn't realized that word had gotten out to the entire hospital that he'd asked her out, but it didn't surprise him. Neither did the fact that everyone seemed to know they were over. Nothing spread through a hospital like reports of a breakup, not even a virus.

What did surprise him though was that all

of his coworkers had rallied to his defense at the perceived threat to his heart. They'd put up walls and shut Stella out in the cold. For a man who had never felt like he truly belonged anywhere, it warmed his heart to see that so many people cared.

Getting the warning that she'd already moved on helped. He'd have completely embarrassed himself if he'd looked up from a patient's chart to see her standing so close to another man so soon. If he'd ground his teeth so much he might need dental work; at least he almost managed to get through their first conversation with the guy present without any reaction.

Key word there being almost.

Then things went a little sideways.

"Stella, I'm going to get the shot from back here since the patient doesn't want to be on camera." The cameraman laid a hand on the small of her back. The touch held a familiarity that said they'd been closer than mere coworkers. Far closer.

The growl that came out of Aiden at that moment would have put a caveman to shame. Stella blushed until all he could think about was throwing her over his shoulder, carrying her back to her apartment and claiming every inch of her.

The cameraman puffed up and Aiden gave him a look that said, “Try it.”

He and the other man stared each other down for a moment before Stella stepped between them. “I think that’s enough from the both of you.”

Neither of them moved.

“Ollie, we should go,” Stella said quietly. She pushed at the guy’s chest until he took a step back. “Wait for me in the hallway, please.”

After he stepped out, she turned and shook her head.

“You are just as guilty as he is of creating a scene, Aiden. I’m going to go before this situation escalates any further. Please let me know if the patient’s imagining looks promising.”

Aiden followed her out of the exam room. As they walked away, side by side, Ollie, as Stella had called him, smirked at Aiden over his shoulder.

Irritation rose up swift and strong. Who did that guy think he was, walking into this emergency department like he belonged here? Acting like he was the king of the castle? No, this was Aiden's domain and he wasn't going to let that slide.

"Hey, Frank," he called to the security guard. "See that guy with the camera there?"

"Yes, sir."

"Don't let him back through those doors again." It might be petty, but Aiden didn't want to see that smug face sneering at him from behind Stella. "Throw him out of here if he sets foot in this emergency department again."

The bitter taste of self-disgust rose hard and swift. He had to swallow it back hard. It wasn't in his nature to be such a petty, jealous Neanderthal. Was he so far gone over Stella that he would act so out of character?

Yes. Yes, he was.

And he hadn't done more than kiss her.

Maybe if he could do more, he'd be able to get her out of his system. He'd just have to get her back in his arms, and hopefully into his bed, so that he could move on.

CHAPTER SIXTEEN

"I BELIEVE I told you already that I didn't care if it was real or fake. Get my footage."

"But Martin—"

"No buts, Stella, I don't care if your hint of a relationship has gone bottoms up. You're running low on time and I'm low on patience. You have to get that footage and quickly."

And that was how she found herself tracking Aiden down to try to talk to him about his continued participation. She dreaded the conversation, even though she slipped away from Oliver to try to have the discussion in private. Aiden and Oliver had taken an instant dislike to one another and she was quite sure she was the root cause.

"Aiden, might I have a word?" she called after him as he came out of one of the trauma rooms.

He stopped walking and gestured in a vaguely positive manner. "I guess."

Since he didn't seem inclined to seek out any privacy, she stood close so that not everyone in the department could hear their chat. "I was wondering if you might find it in you to keep going with your part in the television special."

"No." His curt, swift rejection was on point with his character, if nothing else.

She tried again. "Martin is being quite insistent about it, really. He loved the footage that I'd already sent."

Aiden crossed his arms, leaning slightly closer. Stella's heart rate jumped up at his nearness, and when the movement brought the spicy notes of his cologne over, she had to swallow hard. "If he loved the footage you sent, why'd he send that guy?"

It hit her then that Aiden was completely and totally jealous of Oliver. It wasn't a mere case of rubbing each other the wrong way, but a classic case of envy.

Interesting...

"Cameramen change if the director feels that things aren't moving in the right direction. Admittedly, I never expected Oliver would be one of the cameramen assigned to this project. We haven't worked together at all since before our breakup. I suspect my mother had a hand in his appearance. She has grand hopes of a reunion between us, but that's not what I want."

"What do you want?"

"To fulfill my obligations to St. Matthew's and The Kensington Project and finish this program. The latter would be much easier if you would reconsider your wish to withdraw."

"No," he repeated. "I don't want to fake a romance with you to make some jumped-up director happy. Get your boyfriend to do it."

"Oliver is no longer—"

One of the security guards interrupted their conversation just then. "Hey, Dr. Cook, I thought you'd like to know I escorted that camera-wielding weirdo out of the building for trying to gain access to the emergency department again. Kept him out like you asked."

He walked away whistling.

Stella turned her full attention back to Aiden. She crossed her arms over her chest and glared at him. "You ordered security to keep Oliver out? How's he to get the footage he needs if you won't allow him access to your department?"

"Not my problem." Aiden lifted one shoulder in a way that made Stella crazy. She might have been able to ignore the casual little shrug if it weren't for the sparkle of self-satisfaction she saw in his gaze.

"You most certainly do have a problem. And I think it's jealousy."

"Excuse me?" Aiden's eyes glistened dangerously.

"I enunciated rather clearly." She pushed a finger into his broad chest, trying hard not to smooth her hand across those deliciously firm pectorals. "You sabotaged Ollie because you think he took your place in my life, didn't you?"

"You think far too highly of yourself, Dr. Allen," Aiden argued.

"I think you think quite highly of me as well or we wouldn't be having this conversation."

Aiden stepped closer and put one hand on the wall behind her. His voice carried a dangerous temptation. "What are we going to do about this mutual admiration society we have going on for each other then?"

Stella darted her tongue out to moisten her lips and the small action caught Aiden's attention. His gaze locked on her mouth.

"You are killing me slowly," he said, groaning just before he bent his head down to hers. Stella rose on her tiptoes to meet him halfway, their lips reaching each other in eager anticipation. With her arms around his neck, she returned his kiss with more passion and desire than was really proper for a workplace.

Aiden's hand tugged at her hair, tilting her head so he could deepen the kiss. She sighed as his tongue brushed hers. She wobbled as her knees gave way and he held her against his firm chest, never letting up on the kiss.

He didn't relax his hold on her until the door next to him opened. Then he pulled his lips from her and took a step back.

Stella leaned back against the wall, willing her legs to hold her weight. A couple of employees wrestled a large Christmas tree into the room and maneuvered it into the far corner.

Aiden stood near her, silent, his chest heaving. That kiss had affected him as much as it had affected her, she was sure of it. Although she doubted that he'd ever admit it.

Overhead, a page called out for her to return to the ortho department. "I suppose that's my cue to leave," she said with a smile. "One thing before I go… Oliver and me? Past tense. There's no need for jealousy. Who I end up with in the future has yet to be decided. Have a good day, Dr. Cook."

She walked away before he could say anything else, hopefully leaving him with the image of what could be. With a little effort, and maybe a bit of luck, she'd get the footage she needed and a little bit more.

The knowing look on Stella's face when she dropped that bomb and walked away made Aiden want to punch a wall. She'd all but said, *I know you still have a thing for me.*

That wasn't the part that upset him though. It was the fact that she was right. He did still want her every bit as much as he ever did. He'd illustrated that quite clearly by kissing her just then.

But nothing had changed.

She still didn't want kids and he still had one.

"You know, they say the best way to get over someone is to find someone new."

He looked over at Rita. Her freshly applied lipstick stood out given how far they were into the shift. Stella had been right; Rita did have a thing for him.

"Who said I needed to get over anyone?"

"Your expression did when she walked away." Rita laid a hand on his arm. "How about drinks tonight?"

"I don't think that's a good idea." He searched for the words to let her down easily, because the last thing he wanted to do was to hurt her. But he had zero interest in going out with her. Even though he hated to admit it, as long as Stella was in Toronto, he didn't see himself with another woman.

"It could be fun," Rita said, laying a hand on his arm and leaning her torso his direction. She was a beautiful woman. He should feel… something. Anything. But, he didn't. And that was the problem.

"It wouldn't be fair to you, Rita. I think it's best if I stay single."

"If you change your mind…" She let the invitation trail off. Her meaning was abundantly clear though.

He nodded at her before walking away.

Maybe it really was best for everyone if he stayed single. He hadn't been lying when he said that it wouldn't be fair to Rita. It wouldn't be fair at all to her or to any other woman if he started a relationship right now. Besides, he had Jamie and that's all he really needed, right?

Stella's face flashed into his mind.

She was far more attracted to him than she was Oliver. Anyone could see that.

All he needed to do was find a way to convince Stella that they could share something physical while she was here and leave it all behind when she left. The big question was, who was going to convince his heart to keep the emotions out of it?

CHAPTER SEVENTEEN

FOR THE NEXT WEEK, each day when Stella showed up to St. Matthew's she found Aiden in her path at every turn. When they were filming interviews and a few staged clips, he ran interference with anyone who might interrupt. When she lectured, Aiden attended more lectures than he'd missed, even though he'd seen the same presentation a dozen times now. How many times could he watch her perform her surgical techniques on video while answering questions along the way? Wasn't he tired of it by now?

When she operated, he watched from the gallery. He made sure there were no repeats of the poor behavior she'd dealt with early on. And somehow, he still found more questions to ask. Intelligent questions that showed he'd done his research too.

The constant presence could have seemed too much, but he managed to make Stella feel protected. He managed to toe a line between icy and flirty that nearly drove her mad with wanting him. Some days she wanted to slap his face for the insolence. Others, she wanted to take him back to her apartment and do naughty things to him.

Today was one of the latter days.

She'd been summoned to the medical director's office. Per the email, it was to discuss her progress on the television special and how well she thought the lecture series had gone thus far. She'd brought notes, including numbers on how many surgeons had attended her lectures and how many surgeries had been performed at St. Matthew's Hospital using her technique so far. And she had a list from Martin of the final few scenes he still wanted her and Oliver to film. She had been overprepared for her meeting, as was her normal. Everything had gone as planned. Dr. Stone had even hinted that a position at St. Matthew's Hospital would be Stella's if she only asked.

Then Aiden had walked in.

With one shoulder propped against the wall, and a devastatingly sexy grin thrown her way, he turned his attention to Dr. Stone. His devil-may-care attitude had distracted Stella so much though that she completely lost her train of thought and had to be prompted to find herself again. She finished explaining her progress with heat in her cheeks and a desire to slide under the desk and give up her existence. She'd gone from confident surgeon to spaced-out fangirl over a guy in front of her boss. Recovery from that level of embarrassment might never be possible.

Dr. Stone began talking to them both about the staff Christmas party, but Stella found herself more focused on the way Aiden's fingers drummed rhythmically against his thigh.

"Dr. Allen."

"Hmm..." She pulled her eyes away from Aiden to see the medical director looking at her in amusement. Would she ever live this down? Having only a few short weeks left in Toronto might be her saving grace. If she stayed here much longer, she might actually die of embarrassment.

"Part of the agreement for allowing you to film was setting up this party. We agreed that it will double as a filming opportunity for your special and a nice celebration for my staff. You'll be able to get footage of the doctors 'letting their hair down,' get more interviews as you need and show our employees that we value them. You've come in on budget so far, so good job. I'm still waiting on the final invoices, I believe." Dr. Stone tapped on a piece of paper just in front of Stella on the desk. She gave them both a tight look. "There is another matter. I've heard a few rumors about the two of you, but I expect that you both will be professional. Cordial, even."

"Of course," Stella murmured. She'd really been trying to maintain her professionalism, despite how things might have looked in this meeting.

She glanced over at him, wondering how he'd handle being chastised along with her. His face showed no emotion.

"Do you have any concerns about this, Dr. Cook?" Dr. Stone asked him.

"Not at all." He made eye contact with Stella and she thought she might melt into a puddle of goo at his feet from the intensity. "I'm looking forward to it."

* * *

"I turned in the invoices for the lights and the caterer." Aiden held out a couple pieces of paper. "Copies for your records."

Stella had insisted on having paper copies of everything they'd planned for the party. She might have duplicates or even triplicates of some of it. Organized must be her middle name. Complete overkill, in his opinion, but it seemed important to her, so he'd made sure to get the requested copies for her.

"Thank you," she said. "Any surprises?"

"Nope."

He fell in beside her as they walked toward the cafeteria. Thankfully, Oliver was nowhere in sight, so he had Stella all to himself for the moment. She was different when Oliver was around, not the Stella he'd gotten to know. When the camera was pointed at her, she closed off. Did Oliver even see the real Stella? And if he did, did he appreciate her?

"That's good news. We haven't the budget for surprises." Her accent made him crazy. He could listen to her speak all day about the dullest of topics and never get tired of her voice. The idea of her whispering sweet nothings in his ear as he made love to her kept him up at nights.

He wanted to keep her talking, so he made another comment about the Christmas party. "I wish they'd let us take this off campus though. We could do so much better if we weren't having this party in the hospital cafeteria."

At least they'd had a budget for catering and a cake. Most years the staff party had consisted of cold pizza slices and flat store-brand soda. Stella's program must have rated the upgrade. The higher-ups wouldn't want St. Matthew's Hospital to look bad on camera, after all.

"Hmm..." Stella murmured. "I do agree, of course, but unfortunately we weren't given options on that. So we have to make the best of what we were given. And that's a free location with a lot of seating."

"That's one way to look at it, I suppose." The fact that it was free with a lot of tables and chairs might be the only positive beyond the location making it more convenient for more people to attend.

"I try to focus on the positive whenever I can." Stella raised a shoulder in a little shrug. "There's not much point in focusing on the negatives. I'm far more productive when I look at the bright side."

"The bright side to having the party in the cafeteria is that we aren't having to eat the food, as well." Aiden snorted. "Some days the food looks three days old, other days, it looks like they forgot to kill it before they served it."

Stella wiped away a tear as she laughed. "Hospital food isn't very good, no matter which side of the ocean you're on."

A lock of her dark hair tumbled down into her eyes. Aiden brushed it back for her, tucked it behind her ear. His fingers trailed down along the side of her jaw, savoring the feel of her soft skin under his fingertips. He'd been aching to do so for days.

"You are so beautiful."

When she leaned into his touch instead of withdrawing, he moved in to kiss her. His lips grazed hers, tempting, teasing, waiting for her to tell him to stop. She didn't. His arms slid around her waist and pulled her in closer so that he could deepen the kiss.

"And when you're an outsider dating a medical professional you run the risk of them finding a romance at the hospital," a voice cut in, interrupting an otherwise perfect moment. "Stella and I have been dating for a year and a half. She's been here several weeks now, and as you can see she has found her way into another man's arms."

Aiden looked up.

Oliver stood a few feet away, his camera on a tripod pointed in their direction. He spoke in the direction of the lens. "Romances run rampant in hospitals. Though with the hours they work, most find that they don't have time to meet anyone outside the hospital. Stella and I met on set. It was a whirlwind romance, but I suppose I was more invested than she. I suppose I should be happy that she's not wearing my ring while kissing him."

Aiden looked down at Stella, confusion clouding his mind. He'd never seen a ring on Stella's hand. Not wedding nor engagement. If he had, he'd never have asked her out in the first place. At least he'd like to think he wouldn't have. The chemistry they shared had him doing things he'd never believed he would.

When she didn't say anything, he found himself asking, "His ring?" He winced at the crack of emotion in his voice.

"You didn't know we're engaged?" Oliver asked, glee evident in his voice. Other than sneaking glances at them, Oliver continued speaking to the camera. "We're all set to spend the holidays with my mum and dad too. Wedding planning, you know."

Aiden took a step back.

Stella was shaking her head, tears in her eyes, but she didn't actually deny any of what Oliver had said.

What else could he do but take the man at his word? And though his heart was breaking, he walked away from Stella.

CHAPTER EIGHTEEN

"REALLY, OLLIE?" STELLA finally found her voice. As usual, she froze at the moment of conflict and now it might have cost her everything. From the pain in Aiden's eyes, now wouldn't be the time to chase him down and try to force the conversation. Instead of tracking him down, she spun and stomped over to turn the camera off.

Striding up to her ex-boyfriend, she stopped in front of him and snapped, "Why can't you let me be happy? Is it simply because I'm not with you?"

"It's always been you and me, love." Oliver shrugged. "You simply needed the reminder."

Stella tilted her head and scrutinized him. This wasn't Oliver's idea. He'd never been so calculating. "Who put you up to this?"

"No one," he said, but she heard the lie in his words.

She could see her mother's handiwork behind his actions. "My mum," she said.

"Our mothers thought we should give it another go. My mum's mad about you. And you know yours has always been gone for me, as well." He spoke like their mothers should have supreme say over their lives forever.

Her mother had made far too many decisions over the years without Stella's input. Stella had gone along with a lot for the sake of peacekeeping, but this was too far. No more.

"I don't care if the queen herself thinks we're a perfect match—there is no us. We are over and we will not be giving it another go."

"No?" Oliver asked, looking confused. "But—"

"There are no buts to this situation. I am not interested in giving it another go. I don't want to be with you. Ollie, you aren't a bad guy, you just have no spine. Find someone who loves you enough to stand up for you when your mom tries to push her about. That woman is not me though. Go home. Please."

She walked away, so angry at herself. Interference from her mum was something she should have expected. Debra Allen had been sticking her nose into Stella's business from the time she was born. Even the ocean couldn't provide enough of a barrier to keep the woman from meddling.

Stella's heart ached knowing she'd probably lost Aiden for good now. The look in his eyes when he'd walked away had been so hurt. He'd believed every lie that Oliver had spewed. It had certainly helped that she'd stood there next to him, gaping like a fish and unable to deny the accusations thrown at her. What else could he do but believe Oliver when she'd been incapable of even defending herself?

No, this one was on her. She may not be able to fix things between her and Aiden, but she had to stand up for herself once and for all.

When she got somewhere that afforded her some privacy, she pulled out her phone and called her mother. It was nearly bedtime there, but she didn't care if she woke her. What she had to say could no longer wait. She really should have done this years ago.

The call connected and Stella didn't wait for a greeting. "Really, Mother?"

"Stella, darling, how are you? Is something

wrong? Bit late to be ringing for a chat, not that I'm not happy to hear from you."

Stella strode from one end of the room to another. "It wasn't enough for you to force me into a lifestyle I never wanted, but now you've taken away the future that I do want."

Her mother faked innocence. "How could I—"

"You know exactly what I'm talking about. Having Ollie announce that we're engaged and planning our wedding over the holidays on camera!" Stella paced, her ire rising with every step. "This is your signature move—wait until I'm happy and then ruin everything."

"Stella, this is no way to talk to your mother," her mum huffed, breath loud as it blew over the phone's microphone. "Your accusations are—"

"True. My accusations are completely valid and true." Stella squeezed the bridge of her nose and fought back tears. She really hated confrontation, particularly with her mum, but she'd reached her breaking point. It was time that she stood up for what she wanted in life. "Listen carefully, as I'm only going to say this once. My love life is not under your purview.

My career is no longer under your control. And if you cannot respect those boundaries, then I can and will remove you from my life entirely. I'm done."

So done.

"Goodbye, Mum," she said, hanging up without giving her mother time to say anything else.

Having the entire Atlantic between them was the best thing about their relationship at the moment. If she were on the same continent as her mother, she'd be tempted to move away.

That was it!

Inspiration hit and she knew exactly what she had to do. Things might be over and done with Aiden, but she had one last shot at happiness. And she wasn't going to give up without taking it.

Now she needed to get Dr. Stone on board with her plan.

When Aiden got home with Jamie, his mom looked up from her sewing.

"Is Jamie okay?" she asked, frantically packing her supplies away. "The day care could have called me. I only worked a half day today.

I should have just gone by there and picked him up."

"He's fine, Mom."

She stood and moved closer. Testing the temperature of Jamie's forehead against the back of her hand, she nodded when she confirmed he had no fever.

"Are you sick then?" She treated him to the same temperature check.

"Mom!" He stepped back and out of reach before she decided to do more than check his temperature. "I'm fine."

"You're not." She tilted her head and scrutinized him. "But I'm thinking this isn't a physical ailment."

He sighed and sank down onto the couch with Jamie still in his arms. Hugging his son close, he tried to convince himself that Jamie was all he needed to be happy. Millions of people were happily single. He had been happily single up until a certain British doctor squared off with him at the airport. Now nothing about being single made Aiden happy.

"Jamie, buddy, whatever else happens in this life, I promise you that Daddy will never leave you." He kissed the top of his son's head. "No matter what."

"Is this about Stella?" his mom asked as she sat beside him. Worry lined her face.

"It doesn't matter." Reclining his head back, Aiden closed his eyes. Always so perceptive, his mother. He'd never been able to get much past her. He hated that he was adding stress to her life again.

"I think it does. I've never seen you like this over a woman." She brushed his hair back gently like she used to do when he was a child. "Britney made you feel a lot of things, but I don't think it touched this level, did it?"

Britney had evoked a lot of emotional responses in him. With her, the dominant emotion had been anger, leading to an ever-deepening rage that time had yet to fade. Following the anger had been bouts of disappointment and sadness. Yet he'd never felt as lost as he did knowing that Stella's heart belonged to someone else. With Britney, most of the emotions had been tied to how her actions had affected their son. It had never hurt his heart.

"She's engaged, Mom. And she doesn't..." He glanced down at Jamie. "She doesn't have maternal feelings and I have paternal responsibilities."

Aiden tried to use words he didn't think Jamie would understand. Jamie had been asking to see Stella again as it was and finding out she didn't want to see him might crush the little guy. Jamie had been subjected to more than his fair share of disappointments throughout the years and Aiden wanted to minimize any letdowns that he possibly could.

"But you fell for her anyway."

He closed his eyes tight. "I didn't mean to."

"Most of us don't go out with the intention of falling in love, sweetie. Even when we begin a relationship, we take our time and keep our distance until we can't anymore. It's only when we let our guard down that love has a chance." She took his hand in hers. "I found your father when I had just broken up with my high school love. He asked me out and I couldn't think of anything I wanted to do less. But he was persistent, because he could see a future, even if I was blind."

"You didn't have so many obstacles."

"Maybe not, but no one said love was easy." She put her hand on his chest over his heart.

"You've kept that heart of yours behind a ten-foot wall topped with razor wire. Consider what it was about her that convinced you to let her into your heart."

"I thought she was the one," he said quietly.

His mother stood up. "Jamie, I was thinking that this might be a perfect afternoon to have some ice cream. Can you think of anyone who might want to eat ice cream with me?"

Jamie nodded with a little smile and jumped down to follow her.

"Love finds us when we least expect it, Aiden." She looked down at him and smiled. "If you want her that much, fight for her. Love doesn't come around every day."

Love might not come around every day, but that didn't mean it was meant to be. She was engaged to her cameraman and going back to the UK in less than a week.

Her future wasn't in Toronto or at St. Matthew's Hospital.

And it wasn't with him.

CHAPTER NINETEEN

STELLA STOOD NEAR the doorway watching the doctors and nurses of St. Matthew's Hospital mingle. It was December twenty-third and the Christmas party had arrived. She'd been anxiously awaiting the event to begin and now her nerves were about to get the best of her. If only she were more confident about what she was about to do.

This was her one and only shot to get everything she wanted. There was a chance that it might work, but it was also the biggest risk she'd ever taken in her entire life.

Stella made her way around the room admiring the decor. It was barely recognizable as the utilitarian cafeteria it had been just eight hours before. The tables had been clustered to one side and were covered with red-and-green tablecloths. In the center of each red table sat a small Christmas tree, while the green tables were graced with miniature Santas. Above the tables, tiny fairy lights flashed merrily.

Despite the festiveness of the room, and the general joviality of the crowd, Stella was struggling to be merry. She snagged a plastic wineglass filled with sparkling grape juice just to have something to do with her hands. The mulled wine would have really helped take the edge off her nerves, but they'd strict instructions to make it a no-alcohol party, sadly.

In one corner, there was a cookie-decorating station. Giggling kids of all ages crowded around, jostling each other playfully as they reached for bright icings and colorful sprinkles. Scanning their happy faces quickly, Stella had to bite back her disappointment when Jamie's face wasn't part of the crowd.

The carolers they'd hired gathered along the far wall. Their lovely harmonies added both cheer and ambiance. Stella moved closer to listen. As the melody washed over her, she breathed deeply, trying to steel her nerves for the change that was to come. And it would be coming, no doubt about it. One way or the other, by the end of this party, Stella would know if the changes would fall how she wanted.

To her surprise, people started dancing along to the Christmas carols. The darker middle of the room became an impromptu dance floor as couples swayed and laughed to the music. If only she could let go and dance like that…

Aiden still hadn't appeared. Stella tried to keep an eye out for him, allowing her gaze to drift back to the main entrance every time she caught the slightest movement. If he didn't show up, her plan wouldn't work. She needed him here.

Maybe she could page him?

"Stella! This is amazing!" Gemma wrapped her tightly in a hug. "I didn't think it was possible to transform this toast-bland cafeteria into a practical winter wonderland. The twinkling lights—oh, my heart, are they ever gorgeous!"

It had taken so many strings of lights to create this effect that Stella didn't even want to admit the number. She'd spent half the night stringing up fairy lights so that they could leave off the overhead ones, but the atmospheric effect of the twinkling made it all worth it.

"Have you seen the cake yet?" Stella asked.

"It's too pretty to eat!" Gemma launched into exuberant praise over the cake and the rest of the decorations. Stella tried to pay enough attention to know when she should nod and when a more verbal acknowledgment was required, but she wasn't giving the conversation her all. The bulk of her focus was looking for one specific person.

Just as she was about to give up hope that he'd show on his own, Aiden walked through the cafeteria doors with some of the emergency department staff. Their eyes met. She gave him a slight smile that faded quickly when he looked away without acknowledging her in the slightest.

He wasn't going to make this easy on her.

She swallowed the last of the sparkling grape juice and wished it had been real champagne. A dose of liquid courage would have really helped in that moment. Sucking in a deep breath, she made her way to the microphone that had been set up at the front.

It was now or never.

"Happy Christmas, everyone. Most of you know me by now. I'm Dr. Stella Allen. I've been on loan here from London as part of The Kensington Project. You might also have seen me with a camera in hand or trailing behind me as I film a television special designed to showcase just how hardworking medical workers are, particularly through the holidays."

There was a slight murmur of agreement, but the crowd largely stayed quiet. They'd clearly all sided with the hometown guy. She had her work cut out for her.

"You're probably wondering why I keep blathering on and wishing I'd put a cork in it and let you enjoy your party."

A few yesses chorused back to her.

"I do plan on that—I promise. First, I have an announcement though. Oliver, do make sure you are filming this."

Oliver flashed her a wide smile and a big thumbs-up. The idiot likely thought she was going to announce their engagement just like he'd planned with her mum. He'd remained stubbornly hopeful even as she'd shut him down with every conversation.

Stella gathered her courage. Her next words would change her life.

"The close of this special program marks the realization of a goal for me—to tie my television past with my medical future. Now that I've accomplished that, I'm saying goodbye to television. This will be my last on-air appearance."

The noise in the crowd kicked up.

"Please, quiet, I've a bit more to say and then I'll leave you to enjoy the celebration." When the silence returned, Stella continued speaking. "Television has been good to me in many ways, but it's time for me to move on from that life."

Her heart pounded and there was a rumble of nausea low in her stomach, but she didn't let her nerves stop her. She had one more big revelation, the biggest of all. Seeking out Aiden in the crowd, she made eye contact with him before she publicly declared, "I've also decided to move to Toronto long-term. I hope you'll be welcoming as I join the orthopedic team here full-time in the New Year."

Stepping away from the microphone, she walked across the cafeteria to Aiden. He stood next to the elaborate cake that she'd personally commissioned for this party. His expression was unreadable.

She'd never been more nervous. She'd just told the entire hospital and the world that she was moving to a new country, giving up a large portion of her career, and by walking straight up to him afterward, she'd effectively told everyone that her decisions were all for him. Everything was on the line.

She had no idea where things stood with him, but she was finally following her heart. He might reject her outright, but she'd forever regret it if she didn't try.

Holding out an embarrassingly shaky hand, she asked, "Would you like to dance?"

The cafeteria got so quiet that Aiden could hear Stella's heart racing. Or maybe that was his own. Cheeks blushing a deep rose, she maintained eye contact under his scrutiny and that of the entire Christmas party. Everyone they worked with stood watching, waiting to see if he'd accept her outstretched hand or slap it away in rejection.

It took a lot of courage for her to make a gesture that grand.

There'd been a dozen reasons Aiden hadn't wanted to attend this party. Stella making an extreme gesture to him in front of all of their coworkers hadn't even been on his radar. It was almost too much to process.

He grabbed her hand, but not to dance. He led her away from the cake that had a tiny ice rink on top of it with a miniature couple who had an even smaller little boy with them. Stella had taken care of ordering the cake alone, and now he thought he knew why. The scene on top was meant to remind him of their first kiss.

"I can't do this here." He walked out of the cafeteria, leading her along with him. He was not going to have this conversation in front of all of St. Matthew's and a camera. Far too many nosy coworkers had already been given far too much ammunition to gossip about without them hashing this out in the open.

Stella had just upended everything he'd thought she was going to say. He'd expected a speech, but a *Thanks for a good time—I'll always remember it fondly* sort of goodbye since she was scheduled to leave the next day. He'd expected to hear something about how hard the employees worked and how her program would finally give them a shred of the recognition they deserved.

The last thing he'd expected was for her to say she was staying in Canada. Or that she planned to quit television entirely.

He pulled her into an empty on-call room and slammed the door behind them. The wreath on the door jingled merrily as it fell to the floor from the force of the closure. He spun around and faced her. "Explain to me what just happened?"

"I'm staying," she said simply, as if that were enough of a response that it didn't require further explanation.

"I gathered that." He stared at her, trying to get answers from the expression on her face. The look in her eyes told him that he was missing something, something that should have been obvious, but for the life of him, he was struggling to pinpoint what. Nothing made sense. "What I don't get is why?"

"I rather thought that was apparent."

He stared at her, thoughts bouncing through his head faster than he could fully process. If he was coming to the right conclusion, then he could only think of one reason she might do something so drastic as to uproot her entire career by moving to Toronto and quitting television.

"You gotta give me something here, Stella, because my mind is racing and coming to all sorts of conclusions. I don't know if I'm way off base or if I'm reading the situation right." He swallowed hard when she simply stared at him with one raised brow. "Come on, Stella, give me some answers here."

She shrugged delicately, but the tiniest glimmer of worry cracked through her facade. "I'm moving across the ocean for you. Do you think maybe you could at least meet me part way here?"

Moving closer, he pressed his forehead against hers. He wanted so badly to kiss her and it took every bit of his self-control to keep from doing so. She'd made this big gesture, and it was an amazing thing, but it didn't alter the biggest obstacle keeping them apart.

"I was hoping that's what you meant. But, Stella, you gotta know that nothing's different for me. I'm still a single father. That's not changing."

"I'm aware. When Oliver gave his little speech about us being engaged, and I saw the look on your face, I knew I'd lost you. That's when it dawned on me that I might never see Jamie again either. That realization nearly broke my heart. I never thought I wanted to be a mum, but I do want to be Jamie's mum, or at least stepmum." Her voice choked up with emotion. "I don't think I can walk away from that little boy, or his dad. I've fallen in love with you both, you see."

He wanted to focus on the positives in her speech, he really did, but the mention of her cameraman set his nerves on edge. He didn't want to think of the two of them together, but he had to know. He couldn't move forward with Stella if she remained involved with another guy.

"What about your engagement to Oliver?"

"Nonexistent. Dreamt up as a ploy by my mother to keep me under her control. But that's done, as well. Moving to Canada is my chance to get everything I want."

"And what exactly is it that you want?"

"To be an orthopedic surgeon and live a quiet life with the man I love and his adorable son, assuming you will give me another chance." Her fingers trailed along his jaw before gently tracing his lower lip. "I'm here for the long term. If I have to rebuild your trust, I will do so, even if it takes time."

Aiden couldn't wait any longer. He dipped

down and pressed his lips to hers. He poured all the love he had for Stella into that kiss. Within her embrace, he found hope for the future.

When they broke apart for air, Stella laughed. "Now I really do have to cart everything I own across the ocean."

"And I won't even complain about it this time."

EPILOGUE

Six months later...

"I GOT YOU a pwesent, Stella," Jamie said as he tossed a small, brightly wrapped box into her lap. "It's fwom me and Daddy. Happy birfday!"

"Oh, it's from you both?" She picked up the colorful little package and shook it gently. No rattle. *Hmm.* "Shall I open it now?"

"Yes!"

She carefully peeled the paper off. Her heart rate kicked up when she pulled back the wrapping to reveal a small jewelry box. She popped open the lid and a beautiful diamond ring sat nestled into the velvet lining. She stared at it for a moment, not quite believing what she was seeing.

When she finally looked up, she met Aiden's steady gaze. He got down on one knee in front of her. Jamie wobbled a bit but got down next to Aiden and copied his pose. How cute were they?

Tears welled up in Stella's eyes at the sight.

"Dr. Stella Allen, will you marry me?"

"And me?"

"Yes, of course!"

Aiden took the ring from the box and slid it on to her finger. It was perfect. "I love you, Stella."

"I love you." She leaned forward and kissed him gently. How had she gotten so lucky? "I never expected when I agreed to participate in The Kensington Project that I'd get so much out of it. I thought I'd find a bit of a career boost, make some new professional connections and finally make that TV program. Falling in love wasn't even a consideration, but then I met you."

"Your career didn't quite benefit though," Aiden said, a bit of a wince on his face.

"My medical career will be fine," she reassured him. She'd already settled into a permanent position in orthopedics at St. Matthew's and it had been strongly implied that she'd be in line for the head-of-department position when Dr. Devlin retired. She'd made a quick trip back to the UK to settle her affairs, but she hadn't been able to get back to Canada fast enough. Toronto had quickly become home for her, and it was entirely due to the people. "Getting out of the film industry was a choice I made that I will never regret."

"I can't believe your documentary has already been nominated for an award," Aiden said as he slipped his hand over hers.

"It has been very well received. Of course, it certainly helped that Martin was amenable to cutting out Oliver's ridiculous voice-over and replacing it with the scene where I announced that I was moving to Toronto."

"The farewell to Dr. Stella Allen, former child prodigy, caught a lot of attention."

Giving up her television career hadn't really been a loss, but it had certainly lent a perspective to all that she'd gained. The man sitting at her side was even better than she could have dreamt of. An adorable child sat happily at their feet playing with a toy truck. And across the room were Aiden's parents. The Cooks had brought her into their home with an openness that astounded her. Their visible love for their son and grandson made Stella even more aware of the distance between herself and her parents.

"The personal gains were worth any potential stall my career might face due to the move. I finally feel like I'm part of a family. A real family. Obviously, I had a family, but, oh, I'm not explaining myself very well."

"I get it." Aiden gave her hand a reassuring squeeze. "I spent years wondering why my birth mother abandoned me. Why I wasn't enough. Those insecurities kicked back up when my son was also abandoned."

"You are more than I ever hoped for," his mom said. Love for her family lit up her face. "I hope you know that."

"I do." Aiden flashed his mom a smile. "And you were the best mom that a nine-year-old foster kid could ever hope for. It took me a while to get out of my own way, but I finally realized that family doesn't have to be biological. It shouldn't be something you force out of obligation. Family should be something you choose."

"You are so very right." Stella leaned her

head against his shoulder and sighed happily, knowing she'd made the right choices. "Family is not about blood—it's about love."

* * * * *